To Save a King

To Save a King

by A.D. Fast

Vanwell Publishing Limited
St. Catharines, Ontario

Vanwell Publishing acknowledges the financial support of the Government of Canada through the Book Publishing Industry Development Program for our publishing activities.

Vanwell Publishing acknowledges the Government of Ontario through the Ontario Media Development Corporation's Book Initiative.

Vanwell Publishing Limited
P.O. Box 2131
1 Northrup Crescent
St. Catharines, ON
Canada L2R 7S2
sales@vanwell.com
1-800-661-6136

Produced and designed by Tea Leaf Press Inc.
www.tealeafpress.com

Cover illustration: Margaret Amy Reiach

Printed in Canada

Library and Archives Canada Cataloguing in Publication

Fast, April, 1968–
    To save a king / by A.D. Fast.

ISBN 1-55068-131-1

    I. Title.

PS8561.A84T6 2004   C813'.6   C2004-904112-6

To my mom-and-dad-in-law, Peter & Katharine Fast,
who have always treated me like one of their own.
You are examples of angels on earth.
We should all be more like you.

All around him swords were flying and metal was clanking as knights on horseback ran headlong into each other. The smell of the dark, dingy dungeon was still in his nose, even though he was outside. A full moon lit up the field, staring down like a laughing spectator at this battle. Marvin could feel himself sweating inside the heavy metal armor. He hoped he wouldn't be speared or chopped on his first night in France. Then Louis rode up on a pink horse, carrying muffins...

Marvin McKnight woke up in a sweat. He gazed at his clock—it was eleven-thirty at night. He couldn't believe he had fallen asleep that quickly. He was supposed to be sneaking out of the house after his parents went to bed. Marvin had intended to relax on his bed and go over the plan until he knew his parents were asleep. Instead, he had dozed off. *Some knight I'd be*, he thought as he sat up in his bed, listening for noises in the house.

The house was extremely quiet, just as he had expected. His parents went to bed at eleven o'clock every night. Not just most of the time, but every single night. They were so predictable that it was almost gross. This time, however, Marvin was glad.

As he packed his knapsack with last-minute provisions, his stomach started to churn. He couldn't figure out if it was excitement, fear, or the burrito he ate for dinner. But it didn't really matter. He was meeting Lucas and Nicole at the entrance to the forest whether he was scared to death or sick from cheese and beans. They had to get back to medieval France. The entire history of the world depended on it.

Marvin climbed onto his desk, slid open his window, and stepped onto the roof outside. The heat hit him like a wet towel in the face. It was a deadly hot night in August, and the humidity hung in the air like steam from a hot shower. He could hear the air conditioner humming loudly beside the house.

When he was safely outside, he slid his window closed. He quietly stepped across the roof until he was just above the front porch, where the front lawn rose up into a hill. Then he dropped to the grass below, hitting the ground with a thud and rolling slightly down the sloped yard.

I'm getting good at that, he thought as he hauled himself up off the ground and brushed bits of grass from his shorts. He stayed on the ground for a moment, listening for any noises coming from inside his house. He looked up and down the dark street to make sure none of his neighbors saw him flop off the roof. When he knew the coast was clear, he stood up, hoisted his knapsack over his shoulder, and strolled toward the road.

As Marvin hurried down the dark street, he thought about his dream. All summer, he, Lucas, and Nicole had been waiting to get back to France. Marvin was excited, but over the past week he had started to get nervous, too. He had also been having weird dreams about France. They were always about sword fights and grand battles on the field. And Marvin knew why. They would be fighting in the greatest battle of their lives tomorrow. *But why was Louis riding a pink horse and carrying muffins?* he wondered. *Stupid burritos.*

When Marvin got to the end of his street, he leaned against a tree. The entrance to the forest was right in front of him. Just like last time, he was the first one there. Lucas and Nicole hadn't made it yet.

Marvin looked down the street at the quiet houses lining the road. Some had porch lights turned on. Others were dark and quiet, and Marvin knew that his neighbors were all snug in bed. He sighed heavily. Even though he wanted to go back to France, he was a little bit jealous of the people who slept soundly in their dark houses. They had no idea how dangerous things were just outside their doors.

Marvin, Lucas, and Nicole weren't going to France like normal people. Oh no. They had a much better way to travel, thanks to Marvin's discovery. For deep within the forest was the cave that started it all. The ancient cave had been buried by foliage and hidden for many years until it was discovered fifty years ago. The carving on the wall that looked like nothing but a bunch of strange lines and curves had created a lot of attention. Specialists figured out what the carving meant—it was a phrase. The story was all over the news—at least that's what Marvin's grandpa had told him. Marvin hadn't been born yet.

Grandpa Dave said that for weeks the community buzzed with the story and the mysterious phrase carved into the wall of the ancient cave: *Midnight fly, by twenty-four, back in time no time shall pass. Miss the door in twenty-four and no more.* Everyone had talked about it, but no one knew what it meant. Eventually, the excitement faded and people stopped thinking about it.

Over the years, trees, bushes, and fallen branches covered the entrance. It wasn't disturbed for another fifty years or so. Not until Marvin, Lucas, and Nicole came along. With the help of Grandpa Dave, they not only found the cave again, but they also found the carving. It still didn't make sense to them—until they found three medieval coins in their weird social studies teacher's desk at school last June. That was the part they didn't tell Grandpa Dave. When they followed Mr. LeClair into the forest one night and saw him disappear into the wall, they figured it out. The carving was some kind of portal or doorway. And the ancient coins were the keys.

Marvin smiled, thinking about it. They had done the same thing that night as they were doing tonight. They had snuck out of their houses and into the dark forest and headed straight for the cave. The carving told it all. *Midnight fly, by twenty-four, back in time no time shall pass. Miss the door in twenty-four and no more.*

This was the ancient portal that allowed them to travel back in time to whatever date was on the coin. When they held up one of the coins to the mysterious old riddle carved into the wall, the wall opened up like a giant swirling fireball—only it wasn't hot at all. They simply stepped into the swirling light and landed like a sack of potatoes on the ground—in another time. The date of the coin determined what year they would visit. It was all quite crazy and incredible!

The only problem was that someone else, who was very dangerous, had been using that portal. Someone who was going back in time to commit a horrible crime and disrupt the course of history. That someone was their social studies teacher, Mr. LeClair. And now, Marvin, Lucas, and Nicole had to go back to the year 1450—to the palace of King Charles VII in France to stop a madman from murdering the king.

The crescent moon wasn't giving off much light, and Marvin thought the street looked darker than usual for this time of night. The streetlights hummed in the darkness as he waited for his friends.

The first few times he snuck out at night, he had been nervous. He didn't like being out in the dark so late. He knew it wasn't safe. Now, after all they had been through, the dark night didn't seem to bother him as much. He was more afraid of bumping into Mr. LeClair. They had to be sure that their teacher, who would also be visiting the cave at midnight, didn't see them.

Lucas and Nicole arrived within minutes.

"We meet again, on a dark, starlit night," Lucas said in a low, menacing voice, "going to meet our ultimate doom."

"Get lost," Nicole whispered, shaking her head and rolling her eyes.

Lucas smiled. "I know you're scared, Nic," he said. "You're chicken to go back to the castle. Chicken to see Mr. LeClair. Chicken that we might get caught. Chicken that somebody might find us out." He bent his arms and flapped them like wings, scratching the ground with his feet.

Nicole couldn't help but laugh. Lucas, with his blonde-tipped, spiky red hair, could always make a joke during a tense time. And no matter how much any of them tried to deny it, they were all a little tense. "Oh sure, and you aren't nervous at all, right? I'm telling you, if Mr. LeClair and his guards saw us two months ago snooping around in the castle, we could all be dead. In fact, they may have a trap waiting for us when we arrive," she whispered. "Remind me again why we're going?"

Lucas straightened up and stopped clucking around. "Because if we don't, if we let Mr. LeClair take over the throne of France, history will be changed forever," he answered. He could be serious when he wanted to be. "Mr. LeClair is planning to get rid of the Gutenberg Press, remember? Johannes Gutenberg just invented the first machine ever to print words onto paper. The real King Charles VII is a supporter of the press, but Mr. LeClair isn't. He knows that if books can be printed more quickly in great numbers on a printing press, books will become less expensive and more peasants will have access to them. More of them will learn to read. Mr. LeClair doesn't want the peasants to learn because it would take the power away from the lords and kings. Right now, Mr. LeClair thinks it's great that the lords and kings, who are able to read, have power over the peasants. The rich would stay powerful, and the poor would stay poor. People will never be equal."

Nicole hung her head for a second. "I know. I don't want to live in a world like that. I just know that when we go back this time, it will be very different. We could get stuck in medieval France— if we survive at all."

Lucas stood up as tall as he could and raised his arms in the air. "Fear not! I will protect thee!" he bellowed. Nicole elbowed him in the ribs and told him to be quiet.

"Did you grow again?" Marvin asked, looking up at Lucas. Lucas was much taller than most of the kids in their grade five class last year. Marvin squinted his eyes. It seemed like every week, Lucas Maxwell grew taller and taller.

"You bet. I'm NBA bound, my friend," Lucas answered, smirking.

"Or you're just a freak," Nicole joked.

There was a loud buzz and then a popping sound as the streetlight right beside them went dark. Nicole jumped.

"We'd better get going. Mr. LeClair could be here any time. We don't want to bump into him in the forest," Marvin said, looking over his shoulder to peer down the darkened street. It seemed that not a single soul was awake on this night.

Marvin wished he had his small blue flashlight with him. The beam of light from his mini flashlight would light up a narrow path into the forest. Marvin always kept the flashlight clipped to the belt loop of his pants. He used it all the time, especially since he and Grandpa Dave spent a lot of time in the forest. But Marvin realized as they entered the forest that he had left the flashlight behind in medieval times last June. They would just have to make it to the cave in the dark tonight.

Marvin's eyes quickly adjusted to the darkness of the forest. Moonlight trickled through the leaves of the trees overhead, but it still was almost pitch black. He wondered if they would be able to find their way to the other end of the forest with hardly any light. They had to be extra careful. It was bad enough walking through the forest during the day, never mind in the middle of the night. Luckily, they had been to the cave beyond the rocky ridge many times. Although there were no official paths in the forest, they had worn a path that they were able to follow. Lucas, Marvin, and Nicole had been there many times and usually went to the same spot every time. Their secret cave.

The ground was littered with broken branches, tree limbs, rocks, and stones. Overgrown bushes blocked the way, scraping their legs and arms. Lucas and Nicole followed closely behind Marvin, with Nicole holding onto the back of Marvin's knapsack and Lucas holding onto the back of Nicole's shirt. Marvin almost tripped a few times on fat roots that stuck out of the ground.

Marvin knew the woods better than anyone else. He and Grandpa Dave had hunted for rocks there since Marvin was a small child. Marvin still felt bad keeping all of this from his grandpa, but they had all agreed that the secret of the medieval coin and the portal in the cave had to be kept a secret. If their parents found out what they were doing, they would be in huge, deep, massive trouble. And they would never be allowed to go back. No matter how cool and fun Grandpa Dave was, he surely would have put a stop to them sneaking out to a cave at midnight. Never mind getting sucked into a cave wall.

The ground crunched with every step as they moved deeper and deeper into the woods. The trees and bushes got denser and thicker, and Marvin had to choose the way carefully. It wasn't long before they passed the rocky ridge and finally reached the "little hills," the small hills that lined the far edge of the forest.

Each time an owl hooted, or a small animal made a noise nearby, they turned to look around.

"I think we're being followed," Nicole whispered in a worried voice.

"Don't worry, we're almost there," Marvin said. "Just do the same thing we did last time. When we get into the cave, duck behind the big rock near the back wall. Mr. LeClair will go through the portal at midnight. We'll have one minute to make it through after him. When the coast is clear, we'll jump through."

"Yeah, yeah. The same as last time," Lucas said. "Are you sure Mr. LeClair has been using this cave every night? Hasn't he already found out the information he needs from all those books he reads? Why doesn't he just stay in France already?"

"I don't know why he keeps coming back to our year. All I can say is, he is definitely still using the portal. I've watched the entrance to the forest every night from my bedroom window. I saw him with my own eyes," Marvin whispered.

"Man, you've got to get a hobby," Lucas said.

When they got to the cave, they pushed aside a few branches and crept inside quickly. Marvin could barely see his own hands, it was so dark. They hurried to the huge rock at the back of the cave and crouched behind it so they were completely hidden.

"What time is it, Marvin?" Lucas asked.

"*Shhhhh!*" Nicole hissed. She nodded her head toward the cave opening. Off in the distance they could see a thin beam of light cutting through the darkness, coming toward the entrance. Within seconds, the beam of light entered the cave. It shone right at the carving on the wall. Marvin felt nervous all of a sudden. He kept thinking that the shadowy figure holding the flashlight would shine it directly on them. He was really glad for one thing—that Lucas wasn't trying to make hand animals on the walls in the shadow of the flashlight, like he always did at home.

The light clicked off. They waited in silence for the wall to open up. It was only possible at midnight. Marvin pressed the button on his glow watch to check the time. He was instantly sorry he did that. The flashlight in the cave clicked back on and flicked wildly around the cave. Marvin closed his eyes and held his breath. He couldn't believe he did that. What if they got caught? The light continued to move around the cave. It swept over the entrance and slowly ran along the back wall above them. *Please don't catch us. Please don't catch us*, Marvin chanted silently in his head.

A few seconds later, the flashlight clicked off again. Then came the strange glow they had been waiting for. A dim flicker of light gradually grew into a swirling, glowing, huge round doorway. The person disappeared into the light, which died down as quickly as it had appeared.

Marvin jumped to his feet from behind the rock. Lucas and Nicole stepped out, too.

"Nice one, genius," Lucas said sarcastically.

"I know. I can't believe I did that," said Marvin in embarrassment.

"Yeah, be careful with that watch, Marvin," Nicole said.

They all lined up facing the wall. Marvin was face-to-face with the carving that held the secret. "Okay, you know the drill. Lucas, put your arms around my waist. Nicole, you hold onto Lucas. Who has the coin made in this year so we can get back in twenty-four hours?"

"Got it," Lucas answered. "Actually, I've got a few—just in case."

Marvin held a medieval coin in his hand. He had accidentally taken it from Mr. LeClair's desk on a "fact finding" mission in June. The second coin, the one Mr. LeClair had dropped in the cave the day they discovered his secret, was at Marvin's house.

Lucas, Marvin, and Nicole had to act quickly. They had less than one minute now to activate that portal. It only worked at midnight. Then they would spend the next twenty-four hours in medieval France and would have to return at exactly midnight again. When they got back, no time would have passed. They would have only been gone from home for one minute.

Marvin knew that the task they had before them could affect hundreds of years of history. It was a challenge greater than anything Marvin had ever done. This whole mission was also very risky. Not only trying to save King Charles VII, but just going back at all. Medieval times were very dangerous. And very dirty.

Holding onto the coin, Marvin held his hand up to the carving in the wall. The cold rock tingled beneath his hand. In seconds, the whirling mass of light appeared. Marvin took a deep breath and stepped into the wall. Nicole and Lucas were right behind him.

⇜2⇝

The first thing Marvin saw when he landed on the cold, dirty ground in the dark dungeon of the castle was Louis. Lucas, Nicole, and Marvin were sprawled on the floor after being dumped onto the ground. Louis, squire to Sir Jean the Fierce, of King Charles' court, stood looking down at them.

Firelight flickered from the torches attached to the stone walls. There was an awkward silence. Louis stared at them. They stared at Louis. A prisoner screamed from a jail cell down the hall. Water dripped from a leaky ceiling in the damp dungeon. They stared at one another for what felt like an entire minute. Then Marvin realized that Louis had seen the whole thing.

"You...you lied to me!" Louis said in a thick French accent. He raised his arm and pointed a finger at all three of them. "You are not from Britain…"

Marvin and Lucas got to their feet, still staring at Louis. Nicole stood up slowly.

"You said you were not spies! Or witches! But you lied…" Louis' voice grew louder and louder. Marvin was sure that the guards would come running within minutes. This was not good. They needed Louis to keep quiet, and not just because they wanted to stay out of prison. They needed Louis' help to save the King. He was a key part of their plan. In fact, they couldn't even come up with a solid plan until they convinced Louis to get some crucial information for them. If Louis wasn't on their side, then they were doomed from the start.

Louis started to back away from them, and then he turned to run. Lucas lunged after him quickly. In an instant he grabbed Louis by the shoulders with one arm and covered his mouth. Then he dragged the young squire backwards to the dark hallway that ended at the portal.

"Mmmfffh, mmmffffhhhh!" Louis protested.

"I know, buddy. I'm sorry I have to do this. Just be quiet for a minute and I'll let you go. We can explain," Lucas said. He felt bad treating Louis this way. Louis had helped them when they first arrived at the castle on their last visit. He had shown them around and hid them from the King and the guards. Now Lucas was abducting him and dragging him down the hall. It didn't seem fair.

Louis struggled as Lucas held onto him. Lucas had pinned his arms, and he kept one hand over Louis' mouth.

"Louis, please. We can explain. I swear to you we're not witches. We're not here to harm anyone," Nicole pleaded. Louis seemed to calm down a bit. "Okay. We aren't from Britain, running away from bad knights, like we told you before," Nicole continued. "We are kids who live in the future. In the twenty-first century, actually. We kind of…traveled through time…and now we're here to help the King. The real king, that is."

Louis didn't move. Lucas relaxed his grip a little bit.

"Your king is not the real King Charles VII," Marvin said. "He's an imposter. He's going to kill King Charles when he returns from battle and take over the throne forever. We came here to save the real king."

Marvin looked at Louis. Something in his eyes told Marvin that Louis believed him. "You can let him go," he said to Lucas, nodding.

Lucas let go of Louis and extended his hand. "Sorry, man. I didn't want anyone to hear you shouting and find us," he said.

Louis turned to face Lucas. Slowly his hand rose to the shiny black hilt of the sword he wore in his belt. He backed up against the wall. "What do you mean, you have come from the future?" he asked. "I just saw you come through the wall."

"Well, that's the thing. That wall is a kind of doorway. We held up a coin from this year, 1450, to the carving, and we…" Nicole looked at Lucas and Marvin to finish the sentence.

"…we walked into the wall and landed here," Marvin said.

A strange look flashed across Louis' face. He stared silently at the wall for a long while. "You are speaking of the swirling light?" he asked.

"Yes! You saw it when we landed, right?" Marvin sounded relieved. Somehow Louis seemed to understand about the portal. Marvin could see it in the way Louis looked at them.

"*Oui. Oui*," he said. "I saw the light. I also saw someone else run out of this hallway, just before I found you. That is why I came down here." Although he seemed to understand what they were trying to explain to him, Louis did not loosen his grip on his sword, and his narrowed eyes searched their faces suspiciously.

"Yup. That was him, all right," Marvin said. "That was the imposter who is coming here to take over the throne."

"If I had known, I would have stopped him," Louis said.

"Oh no you wouldn't have," Marvin corrected him. "That was the person pretending to be the King. You would have been in huge trouble."

"This is too much." Louis frowned and rubbed his chin. "So you say you are from the future?" he asked with disbelief. "Why have you come here, then? And why did you leave last time? I thought I would never see you again."

"We could only stay for twenty-four hours last time. We had to leave at midnight. We couldn't tell you because...well...we didn't know *what* to tell you. This time, we have come to help you," Marvin answered. "The man who is calling himself King Charles VII is not the real king at all. He is an imposter."

"*Non.* This cannot be. Why do you say such lies against His Majesty?" Louis asked.

"Because we read it in our history books. The real King Charles is supposed to be away at battle from July 31, 1449, until the end of the battle of Cherbourg on August 12, 1450. That's today. So the real king couldn't have been here for a few months already," Marvin explained.

"You learned this in a book?" Louis asked.

"Yes," Marvin answered. "And remember, you told us when we were here before that the King was not himself lately."

"*Oui.* And he has kept his most trusted friend in prison," Louis added.

"Jacques is still locked up?" Lucas asked. "The King had just thrown him in jail when we were here last time. That was, like, two months ago." Jacques Coeur had helped Marvin, Lucas, and Nicole save Louis from a deadly joust. He was a very kind man and a very good knight.

"Well, now we know why Jacques is still in jail. The King is not the real King Charles VII, and Jacques knows it," Nicole said.

Louis didn't say a word. He looked terribly confused and terribly upset.

"So, will you help us?" she asked.

"I do not know. I…I am confused. The future. I cannot believe…" He shook his head.

Lucas held out his hand, the coin from modern times lying in his palm. "Would this convince you?" he asked.

Louis inspected the coin closely in the torchlight. He took a deep breath and shook his head again. "I want to know everything. I want you to tell me about where you come from. I want to know everything about the future."

Marvin looked over at Lucas and Nicole. No one knew what to say.

Louis began to pace. "You must know everything about France's future. You must know hundreds of years of history! You must tell me all about it!" he said. His eyes grew wider and wider with excitement.

"Louis, we'll tell you about life in the future, but first we have to save history," Marvin said. Marvin knew that he could not tell Louis everything about the future. There are some things a person should not know. They could not risk Louis telling anyone about a life-saving invention or about the outcome of wars. That could change history. But they could probably tell him about kids in the future, and what it is like to go to school, and what houses look like. *That couldn't hurt, could it?* Marvin wondered. He realized that he would have to think long and hard about what information he could give to Louis.

"Save history? What do you wish from me?" Louis asked. He spoke English very well for a squire in medieval France.

"Louis, we need you to help us hide out for a while. We might also need help getting some information about the imposter king's plans," Marvin answered.

Louis stared at Marvin for a moment. Then he spoke slowly. "You are my friends, and I will help you stay safe. As for information about the King...I do not know," he said.

Marvin nodded his head. "Okay. That's a start. I know it sounds a little crazy and it's hard to believe that the man you think is your king is actually a deadly imposter. If you can just help us stay safe, that's great. We can't expect you to help us more than that."

"Then you understand. *Bien.* Now, what do you wish to do first?" Louis asked.

"Well, for starters, we'll need those clothes again," Lucas said. On their last visit, Louis had given them the clothes of prisoners who had "left the building." Without the clothes, they couldn't have blended in with the townspeople.

"I believe you took them with you," Louis said. Marvin nodded his head. Last time, they had barely made it through the portal on time. They had arrived home in stinky medieval clothes covered in moat water.

"Oh, that's right," Lucas said. "Sorry."

"Not to worry. I will find you all something else to wear," Louis said. He walked down the dark hallway toward another hall that held prison cells.

"Can you get me something a little more manly?" Lucas asked. "I really don't look good in tights." Nicole elbowed him. Lucas turned to her and shrugged his shoulders. "What?" he asked.

A moment later, Louis was back with an armful of clothes. Lucas, Marvin, and Nicole each hid in a different dark corner of the dungeon and changed. When they came back out, they smiled at one another. Once again, the boys were given long pants that looked like tights, leather boots that went all the way up to their thighs, and long tunic shirts. They had each tied a belt around their waist. Nicole was wearing a long brown dress with an apron.

They gave their modern clothes to Louis so he could hide them. Marvin's knapsack was hidden in the pile of clothes.

"Now hurry. We have to get you out of here," Louis said when he returned. "And you must stay out of sight at all times."

"Why?" Marvin asked. He wanted to look around the castle some more, like they did last time.

"Because..." Louis unrolled a piece of paper and held it up. The writing was in French.

Nicole, the French expert and all-around smart person, read it out loud. "His Majesty the King, Charles VII of France, does decree on this day, August 12, 1450, that whoever captures three spies from a distant land will be given thirty gold coins and must surrender the spies immediately for execution." Then she gulped and turned to look at Lucas and Marvin.

"There's a price on our heads," she said.

3

The blood drained from Marvin's face. He didn't want to be executed. This mission was going to be dangerous enough. Now the decree made it even more dangerous. People would be watching out for them, looking to capture them and receive the reward of thirty gold coins. And then heads would roll. Their heads.

"Hey, that decree said 'three spies' from another land. It didn't say anything about the spies being kids," Lucas said. He had a good point. Last time, they had been chased in the castle by the King's guards, but apparently the guards hadn't realized that the spies were children.

"It's because I am tall, dark, and handsome," Lucas said. "I look like a teenager. Totally. Maybe even a man."

"Please. You are medium height, red, and homely," Nicole said. She smirked.

"Again, she cuts me like a knife. Really, Nicole, you must start being nicer to me." He grinned his dimpled grin at her. "I mean, I am the looker of this trio."

Nicole rolled her eyes. "Whatever. Anyway, what are we going to do? We can't hide down here all day. We have to figure out how Mr. LeClair is going to get rid of the King. We can't do that by hiding out."

"I have an idea. Follow me, *s'il vous plaît*," Louis said. He bowed, allowing Nicole to pass. She blushed. Lucas rolled his eyes.

They walked quietly along the damp, darkened hallway. Nicole stopped at a set of stairs that they had used before. The stone staircase led up into the castle.

"*Non*," Louis whispered. "Not this time. Even at this late hour, there are people working in the kitchens, and there are guards on duty. I must sneak you out another way." He led them to the end of the hall and pointed up to the ceiling. There was a large wooden trapdoor right above them. It looked like it was made of thick slabs of wood lashed together.

"What is this?" Lucas asked. "And where are the stairs?"

"This is an old trapdoor. And there are no stairs here because we are not supposed to use it," Louis answered. "Now, we will heave each of you one by one through that doorway. I will come up after you."

"But how will you get up?" Nicole asked.

"You will see, *mademoiselle*," he answered.

"Where does the trapdoor lead?" Marvin asked.

Louis shot him a devilish grin. "It will lead you outside."

Louis and Lucas stood on either side of Marvin to give him a boost. Marvin braced himself as the two boys hoisted him into the air by his feet so he could reach the trapdoor. He tried to push up the trapdoor, but it was surprisingly heavy. Marvin grunted as he pushed with all his might. Finally, he managed to lift the door and slide it over a couple of inches.

"Dude, hurry up!" Lucas grunted. "This is killing me!"

"I'm trying. This thing is heavy," Marvin whispered. He took a deep breath and pushed again with all his might. The door slid over to create an opening large enough to climb through.

"Okay, here goes," he called down. He grabbed the edge of the opening with both hands. "Okay, go!"

Louis and Lucas gave his feet a final hoist up as high as they could lift him. Marvin felt like a human elevator. "Going up," he said.

He pulled himself up through the hole and found himself outside, kneeling on the ground. He looked around the dark, starry night. The castle loomed behind him, dark and quiet. He could not see much else around him, since it was just past midnight and the castle did not have lights. The air smelled fresh and clean, like it did after a day of rain. Marvin suddenly realized that his knees were wet and dirty.

He scrambled to his feet and turned back to the trapdoor just as Nicole was pulling herself up. Lucas came next. Even though he only had Louis propping him up, he climbed through quickly.

"How are you going to get up here?" Marvin whispered down to Louis.

"The stairs," Louis answered.

They watched as Louis disappeared from view down below. Moments later he walked out the castle door and joined them outside.

"Why didn't we just do that, too?" Lucas asked, annoyed.

"Because we cannot risk anyone seeing you in the castle," Louis answered.

"Wow, so what is this trapdoor used for, anyway?" Marvin asked. "Isn't it dangerous to have a way into the castle from outside like this?"

"Many years ago there was an outdoor kitchen on this spot. Food was stored in the dungeons under the castle to keep it cold. In time, a kitchen was built inside the castle, and the outdoor kitchen was torn down. Most people forgot about this door, but I did not," Louis answered.

"But what do you use it for?" Lucas asked.

Louis smirked. "For sneaking in and out of the castle."

"Sneaking in and out? Why would you need to do that?" Nicole asked.

"I do not need to do it anymore. But I did use it as a child," he answered. Before anyone could ask him why, he changed the subject. "Now, we must place the door back on the opening so that it is not found by others. You will know to use this door if you need to come into the castle. I must tell you again, however, that you should avoid the castle as much as you can. The King is looking for spies. Your lives are in danger."

"You don't have to tell me twice!" Lucas said. "If the King has issued a warrant for our arrest, we have to stay away."

"Yes, but where will we go?" Nicole asked.

"Do not worry. I have just the right place for you," Louis said.

Louis led them through the courtyard toward
the drawbridge, where two guards stood ready.
Marvin felt butterflies in his stomach. The guards
wore heavy red tunics with blue and gold
embroidery, and each had an armor plate strapped
to his chest. The large, shiny shield in one hand and
glimmering sword in the other told Marvin that
these guys meant business. There was no way they
were getting across the moat surrounding the castle
by using the drawbridge.

Louis put out his arm to stop the three friends
from walking any farther. He looked around for a
moment, and then he gestured for them to follow
him another way. They went across the courtyard
toward the stone wall surrounding the castle and
the courtyard. There were many tall, narrow slits

along the stone wall. Marvin knew from studying medieval times in school that the slits were called arrow loops. From the outside, the slits were so narrow that no one could sneak through. They were wider on the inside, however, so that a person could stand inside the wall and shoot out of the arrow loop. Marvin wondered why Louis would take them there. None of them were small enough to squeeze through an arrow loop.

Louis stood in front of one of the slits for a few moments. Then he waved for them to follow him in. He had removed some bricks from around the narrow outside opening and slid a long wooden plank across the moat. They could barely see the plank in the darkness. When Lucas, Marvin, and Nicole were close enough, he explained his plan.

"Move slowly and carefully. We must slide along the plank on our bellies. Do not move too quickly or make any noise. If the guards hear you, they will shoot you from above," he said in a voice so quiet they could barely hear him. "The last of you out must replace the bricks."

Marvin gulped and looked at Nicole and Lucas. They looked concerned, too, but Marvin knew that they had no choice. They had to get out of the castle grounds before they were seen.

Marvin followed Louis across the plank, sliding slowly along the wood. He moved as quietly as he could, even when he felt a sliver of wood pierce the skin of his left leg. Lucas was close behind. Nicole came last. She fitted the bricks back around the arrow loop like a giant puzzle before she slid across the plank. Luckily, no one fell into the stinky moat.

When they were all back on land again, they helped Louis pull the plank across and stash it in a nearby cluster of trees. They would have to use it again later to get back into the castle.

"Isn't that a little bit dangerous? I mean, if *we* can get back in, can't *anybody* get back in? What's the use of a narrow opening if people can just take it apart and squeeze through?" Lucas asked. Marvin agreed. It didn't seem very safe.

"Yes, it is dangerous. And I am trusting you with this secret. If invaders found out about it, they would be able to get inside. Let us all hope that invaders do not find out about it," Louis answered. "For me, it has been a blessing."

"Wow. You rebel, you," Lucas said teasingly.

Marvin was shocked that Louis would break the rules like that. He kept wondering why Louis would need to sneak out of the dungeons, and now out of the castle grounds. Why didn't he just use the drawbridge at the front gates?

Louis led them away from the castle and down the rolling hillside. At the bottom of the hill was a broad field. When Marvin looked back, the castle seemed dark and quiet. He didn't trust what he saw, though. Louis had told them to be very quiet and not to run because there may be guards patrolling the castle wall or watching from the "windows" in the turret, the rounded tower. No one fired arrows at them, and no armies of knights came after them, so Marvin figured they were safe.

They walked in the starlit night for a long while. Marvin was starting to feel very tired.

"So…can you tell us where we're going?" Lucas asked.

"I am taking you to a village nearby. I have a friend there. He and his family may be able to hide you for a while," Louis said.

"Really? Where will they hide us? And what are we supposed to tell them? That we're your long-lost cousins?" Lucas asked.

"*Non*, I do not have cousins. They will know that. Instead I will simply say that you are my friends and you need help," Louis answered. He was deep in thought.

"But why would they want to hide us if they know that the King has placed a price on our heads and they could make money by turning us in?" Lucas questioned.

"Hopefully, they will not know about the King's decree. It was only sent to the King's court. The peasants cannot read, anyway. And the King does not spend time with the peasants. He only sends his tax collectors to collect the King's payment," Louis answered. "I must warn you: if the King's men come after you, you will have to leave. I do not wish to put my friend or his family in danger. And while you are there, you will be working for your keep."

"Er…working for our keep? What is that supposed to mean?" Lucas asked.

"Yeah, Lucas doesn't like to do work, Louis. He could get his nails dirty," Nicole added.

"Oh, sure. Just because I didn't want to help your dad gut a pile of fish at a family camping weekend, you think I'm afraid to get my hands dirty? Forget about it. I can work as hard as the next guy. Check out these pipes," Lucas said. He made a fist and bent his elbow to flex his muscles.

"Looks like a skinny chicken leg to me," Nicole said, giggling.

"Can a chicken leg do this?" he asked, and he wrapped his arm around Nicole's waist and squeezed tightly. "Chicken death grip!"

"Ahh, let me go!" Nicole squealed. She laughed and wriggled free.

"Will you guys be quiet?" Marvin said. "We don't want to wake up everyone in the village."

Louis had stopped walking. "You should not treat a young lady like this," he said seriously.

Lucas, Marvin, and Nicole looked at one another. "I'm fine, Louis. We always joke around like this," Nicole said.

"Are you certain? Because I will protect your honor," he offered.

"Her honor? She has no honor. She hangs out with me!" Lucas said, shrugging his shoulders.

Marvin saw the concerned look on Louis' face. He knew that in medieval times, men and women were treated very differently than they were in modern times. And women were not always treated like friends. "What he means is that Nicole does not need to be protected from Lucas because they're friends. Where we come from, it's all right for boys and girls to be friends and joke with each other," he explained.

Louis started to walk again. "Fine. I just do not like to see a lady insulted," he said. Nicole smiled and blushed.

"That wasn't insulting. Insulting is when I call her funny-looking and make jokes about her hair and her shoes, and when I call her—"

"*Shhh*," Marvin hissed, elbowing Lucas in the side. "He doesn't get it. Knights are trained to defend castles and ladies' honor. He might find it his duty to fight you."

"Get out! Seriously? You don't think…? Maybe he likes Nicole, I mean, maybe he *likes* likes her. You know what I mean?" Lucas asked.

Marvin shrugged and looked back. Nicole and Louis were walking side by side, and Nicole was laughing. "I don't know, but having a boyfriend who lived hundreds of years in the past would really stink," he answered.

Eventually Marvin could see the outlines of small buildings in the distance. As they walked closer, the cottages became clearer. Small groups of square or rectangular wooden buildings were grouped together. Large plots of land nearby were planted with wheat or other crops. Small fenced areas kept the pigs and sheep from running wild. The village was surprisingly quiet.

"*Shhhh,*" Louis hushed as they approached the village. "We will soon be at the home of my friend. Agree with whatever I say and speak as little as possible," he whispered. He gave an extra long glare to Lucas.

Lucas stared back and shrugged his shoulders. "What?" he whispered.

Louis led them toward a small cottage that had a pigpen and another small building nearby. Lucas, Marvin, and Nicole followed him toward the home. Louis stopped walking, but Marvin kept walking toward the front door.

"*Non!*" Louis whispered loudly. "Follow me."

He led them to the smaller wooden building beside the pigpen. He removed the metal pin from the door and quietly pulled open the enormous wooden barn door. When they were safely inside, he pulled the door closed again. It was even darker in the building than it was out in the dark night.

Marvin was immediately hit by the horrible stench inside. Instantly, he knew where they were. Hay crackled underfoot, and a large, brown beast lay in one corner. Bales of hay lined the walls, along with hoes, scythes, and other farming equipment. His eyes watered from the smell of manure.

"We're hiding in a barn?" Lucas asked quietly.

"This will be more comfortable than the dungeons…or the executioners' quarters, *non?*" Louis answered. "You will be safe here."

He walked toward a square window high up in the wall. A rope hung down from the windowsill and disappeared outside. Louis picked up the rope and pulled on it three times. A few moments later, the barn door inched open.

❧ 5 ❧

Marvin quickly hid behind a stack of baled hay, his heart racing. *We haven't even made our plan yet. We can't be caught so early on,* he thought. Slowly, a figure slipped in through the barn doors.

"Bonjour!" Louis said quietly.

"Ah, bonjour!" the person said. Marvin squinted and stood up, certain that this was not someone who was going to get them into trouble. After a few moments, Marvin realized it was a boy. He looked about eleven years old—no older than they were.

"How did he know we were in here, Louis?" asked Marvin.

Louis smiled. "We have a system. The rope that I pulled is very long. It goes from this barn all the way into Pierre's home. There it is tied to a wood block. When I pull on it, he can hear the wood block move and knows I am here. We have been using that rope since we were children."

"Qui sont ces personnes?" the boy asked after hearing Marvin in the shadows. Marvin didn't know French as well as Nicole, but he understood that the boy was asking Louis who they were.

Louis and the boy spoke for a while in French. Finally, Louis turned to speak to Lucas, Marvin, and Nicole in English. "Do not worry. This is my friend Pierre. I have told him that you are my friends from Britain and that I am trying to help you hide from someone. He said you may stay here," Louis said.

"Oh, thanks," Marvin answered, smiling. He walked closer to Pierre, but even when he stood right in front of him, Pierre did not look at Marvin. He seemed to be looking past Marvin, somewhere over his shoulder. Marvin looked over his shoulder, wondering what Pierre was looking at. Then Marvin glanced at Louis with a look of concern.

"He cannot see you," Louis said, answering Marvin's silent question.

"Oh. Of course. It's very dark in here," Marvin answered. He waved his hand in front of Pierre's face. "Hey, over here," he said.

"Non, he cannot see you. He is blind. Pierre was ill as a child, and he lost his eyesight," Louis explained. He said something quickly in French, and Pierre laughed.

"Oh, jeez. Sorry. I didn't mean to...sorry about that," Marvin mumbled. He felt horrified. He couldn't believe he had waved his hand in front of a blind person like that. He hoped Pierre wouldn't hate him for it.

"Marvin!" Nicole said. Then she started speaking to Louis and Pierre in French.

"This...is...fine," Pierre answered with a thick French accent. Marvin figured that Louis had been teaching Pierre a little bit of English. Pierre smiled and put out his right arm to shake Marvin's hand.

"So, what about Pierre's parents? Won't they find us here?" Lucas asked. He walked over to a pile of hay and sat down. The cow mooed in the corner. "Don't worry, dude. We aren't staying long," he said, more to the cow than to Pierre.

"It is Pierre's job to look after the barn, the chickens, and the cow. His family does not come in here often. We will tell his parents that you are friends of mine," Louis answered. "Tomorrow you can help them tend the fields. There is plenty of weeding to be done before the crops are ready in the fall. They will be happy to have you work for them."

"Okay," Lucas said. "I can weed a garden."

Louis smiled and started speaking with Pierre in French.

Nicole leaned over to Marvin and whispered, "Um, Marvin, shouldn't we be working on our plan for saving the King instead of weeding the garden?

I mean, as much as I want to help Pierre's family, we don't have much time before we have to kick some royal imposter butt. And we don't even have a plan yet."

"I know," Marvin whispered back, "but we won't get anywhere if we can't convince Louis to help us. We'll help Pierre's family as a show of good faith. We need to get on Louis' good side so that we can get him to join the team and get us that information we need."

Nicole frowned. "Okay, but—" She stopped talking when Louis turned back to them.

"Hey, Louis," Lucas piped up. "One important question. Where are the chickens?" He looked around the barn, waiting to be attacked by mean pecking menaces.

"Do not be silly. Chickens do not live in a barn," Louis said, laughing.

"No, they would be in a chicken coop, genius," Nicole said to Lucas.

"*Pardon?* They live in the house, of course," Louis corrected. He pointed in the direction of the little cottage that Marvin almost walked into earlier.

"No way!" Lucas laughed. "Inside the house? With the family?"

Louis and Pierre didn't seem to find that even the slightest bit funny. "But of course. They roost in the rafters, not on the ground. Why do you laugh?"

Lucas quickly got control of himself. "Nothing...I guess. I'm just picturing my mother with chickens sitting up near the ceiling of our house. She would freak out!" He paused for a minute. "You know, that would really be funny." He stared off for a minute.

Nicole rolled her eyes. "Don't listen to him. He doesn't get out much," she said. "So, what do we do now?"

"You can sleep here for the night. I will stay, also. Since Sir Jean the Fierce is away at battle, I will not be missed," Louis said.

Marvin felt bad for Louis. He knew that a squire's duty was to assist a knight and to learn from him. With Sir Jean away, Louis was missing out on his training and felt left behind. Even so, Marvin couldn't understand why Louis would want to go off to battle, especially the Hundred Years' War. The final battle, the Battle of Cherbourg, was being fought right now. Many French people would die in the fighting. Marvin knew he couldn't tell Louis all of this. Too much knowledge of the future would probably scare him. Marvin just hoped that Sir Jean, to whom Louis had devoted his life, would return from the battle. He was glad the history books didn't mention Sir Jean by name. He would have felt awful knowing that something bad was going to happen to Sir Jean. It would have been a terrible secret to keep.

Louis removed his tunic and laid it near a bale of hay. The white shirt underneath had a collar and long sleeves. It was buttoned all the way down.

Marvin took a closer look at the tunic. There was a colorful crest on the left chest. Gold thread spelled the words *"Sujets fidèles, pour la gloire."*

"Wow," Lucas said. "That crest on your tunic. I didn't see it last time. What's it for?"

Louis smiled proudly. "Some of the King's trusted servants have been given this crest. It bears the King's coat of arms and the motto he gives to his most loyal subjects. I was given this crest shortly after the joust you attended with me."

"What does it mean?" Marvin asked. He stared at it long and hard. Every noble family had their own coat of arms. Blue, red, yellow, green, and gold thread created the pattern of a lion with curved paws on a gray shield. The words were written beneath the crest.

Louis was trying to grasp for the right words when Nicole interrupted him. "Loyal followers, chosen for glory," Nicole read.

Louis smiled and bowed toward Nicole. *"Oui, c'est correct,"* he said. He ran his hand through his collar-length, wavy brown hair. "You are very smart, Nicole."

"Merci," she answered shyly.

"Merci!" Lucas imitated her in a high voice, batting his eyelashes.

Nicole reached over to slap him. Then she flicked her long, brown hair over her shoulder. "Be quiet, Lucas. You're just jealous that I can fit in around here better than you can."

"Jealous? I'm not jealous," he answered.

"Anyway, that crest is really cool," Marvin said to Louis. "You must be honored to have it. Do all of the knights and squires in King Charles' court have one? Is it like a badge of honor?"

"I guess it is, perhaps. But not everyone has one. That is what makes this so special. Some of the King's bodyguards do not even have one, and yet it was given to me. A few others received the crest at a feast a few weeks ago, as well. The King himself sent this to me," he answered proudly. Then his smile faded. "But you say he is not the King at all. Correct? I am sorry to say, I do not know if I agree with you. He has not been himself, but he cannot be a complete imposter. Surely someone would know."

"Sorry, buddy," Lucas said. "According to the history books, King Charles VII has body doubles— look-alikes—that are part of the Scots Archers, his bodyguards. The real King Charles the VII is away at the battle of Cherbourg until tonight. The king living at the castle is not the real king."

Louis reached out and traced the pattern on the crest of the tunic lying on the hay. He shook his head sadly. "But why? Why would anyone do such a thing as to impersonate a king? He will be put to death for certain when the real king returns."

"Not if he doesn't get caught," Marvin said.

"What do you mean?" Louis asked.

"Well, if the real king is not allowed to return, say maybe he mysteriously disappears, then the imposter king will never get caught," Marvin explained. "That's why we came back. We think the imposter is planning to kill the real king as he returns from battle. We need your help to intercept him. We have to save the real king, or history could change forever."

Louis didn't answer. He simply shook his head slowly. "I am sorry, Marvin," he said quietly. "I still cannot believe this. I will keep you safe, but I cannot help you with your plan to attack a king."

After a few hours of sleep, Marvin woke up to bright sunlight streaming in through the barn window. The cow quietly chomped on hay in the corner of the barn. Marvin rubbed his tired eyes and looked over at the cow, which simply stared back at him with a bored expression. "Good morning," Marvin whispered.

Lucas thrashed around in his sleep. Marvin could hear him mumbling something about sandwiches. Then Lucas suddenly sat up, his eyes bugged wide open. He made a *pthththththt* noise as he spat hay from his mouth.

"Hey," he mumbled when he noticed that Marvin was already awake.

"Hey," Marvin said quietly. "Did you sleep at all last night?"

"Mmmmmmm, a little bit, I think," Lucas answered. He yawned and stretched his arms high above his head. He looked over at Nicole sleeping on a bed of hay that she had carefully piled before going to sleep. He smiled and raised his eyebrows to Marvin.

"Don't do it," Marvin warned.

"Oh, but I must," Lucas whispered. He loved a good practical joke. He quietly crept over to where Nicole was sound asleep and picked up a piece of straw. Then, crouching down near her face, he tickled her cheek with the end of the straw, making her face twitch. She began to mumble and then flick her face with her hand. Lucas tried to muffle his laughter. Then, without warning, she sat up and flung her arms around wildly, hitting Lucas repeatedly in the face. Lucas tried to raise his hands to defend himself, but he was being smacked this way and that. Finally, Nicole woke up.

"Ow!" Lucas complained.

Nicole looked confused for a second and then focused on Lucas. "You goof!" she said. "I was dreaming about a sword fight when you woke me up. You scared me half to death. It's a good thing I didn't actually have a sword in my hand, or you would look like a cut-out snowflake."

"A cut-out snowflake? That is the scariest thing I've ever heard, Nic. Wow. You're really tough," Lucas said. "And good morning to you, too, sunshine!"

Nicole giggled and shook her head. She smoothed her long, brown hair and straightened her short bangs.

"I bet you wish you had your pink brush and that silver bag of hair thingies," Lucas teased her.

"Do you memorize every little thing in people's houses, or what?" Nicole asked.

"I have a keen eye for detail, my friend. You can't slip anything past me," he answered smugly.

"Yeah, except a French test. That slips waaaaaaay past you," she answered.

Lucas threw a handful of hay at Nicole, but she turned away. When she finally stood up, she looked around the barn. "Hey, where's Louis? I thought he was staying last night."

Lucas, Marvin, and Nicole looked around the barn. Louis was nowhere to be found.

Lucas shrugged his shoulders. "I don't know. Maybe your snoring scared him away," he said.

"Or your feet. Do us all a favor and put those boots back on," Nicole said.

Just then the barn door swung open. Louis and Pierre came inside, Louis carrying a tray and Pierre carrying a bucket. "Good morning," Louis called as he placed the tray on the ground in the center of the barn.

"Oh, there you are," Nicole said. "We were getting worried for a second. Good morning." She walked over to the tray and sat down on the ground, gathering her long skirt around her.

Marvin and Lucas joined her in the circle, along with Louis and Pierre.

"We have breakfast," Pierre said, smiling. Marvin could tell that he was proud of himself for speaking English.

"Thank you," Marvin said. He looked down at the wooden tray on the floor. There was dry bread, a tiny piece of butter, and water.

"What? No 'Happy O's' and orange juice?" Lucas asked jokingly.

Pierre's face dropped. "This is all," he said. He turned to Louis and spoke in French.

"Pierre said his family has little food, and although he would like to offer more, this is all he could offer you," Louis said coldly.

"I'm just kidding. Really. This is very kind of you to feed us. Thank you," Lucas said. He looked at Marvin and mouthed, "I was just kidding." Marvin nodded.

"Yes, this is very nice," Nicole said. Pierre smiled a little. He passed around hunks of bread for them to take and one large mug filled with water for them to share.

When the tray was completely empty, Marvin got up and looked out the small hole in the wall that served as a window. The sun was barely up, and he could hear roosters crowing in the distance.

"So, what do we do today?" Marvin asked.

"I work in the fields," Pierre answered. "You can stay here."

"No, we'll help you," Lucas said. "What do we need to do? Weed the garden a bit and then put the tools away? That shouldn't take very long."

Louis said something to Pierre in French, and they both laughed.

"Thank you, Lucas. Pierre and his family could use the help," Louis said. "I have spoken to Pierre's parents this morning. They have agreed to hide you, but only for today, and only if they are not in danger. Just do not do anything that might cause them trouble."

They walked out into the sunlit morning and saw the village clearly for the first time. Small wood and mud huts dotted the land, their hay-thatched roofs rustling gently in the fresh morning breeze. People bustled around the cottages. The smell of flowers and grass floated on the air, a welcome change to the foul smell inside the barn. Some villagers kept their cows and sheep in barns, while others kept their livestock inside their small houses. They would lead the animals outside to graze.

Women in long dresses with kerchiefs on their heads busied about tending animals, sweeping out the small houses, or looking after small children. Many people carried gardening tools toward the fields. One man threw a rotting vegetable at someone who was locked up by his ankles and wrists in a large wooden structure.

"What is that?" Nicole asked, pointing to the strange structure. The man's head rested just above the wooden plank, while his feet and hands stuck out through holes in the wood. A large lock dangled from one end of the wooden planks.

"Those are the stocks. And that is Franc Baker. Pierre told me he was caught selling bread at less weight than he said it was. He has been locked in the stocks overnight as punishment. I am sure the lord of the manor will free him today," Louis said.

"The lord of the manor?" Nicole asked. She looked around the small village. "Who's that?"

Marvin knew the answer to this one. "Kings give land to lords in exchange for crops, money, and support in battle. The lord, in turn, allows peasants to live in villages on the land in exchange for crops. The peasants must farm the land and pay rent to the lord, who lives in a large manor in town. The lord of the manor is like the boss. He reports back to the king." Marvin was proud of his knowledge of medieval times.

"Oh yeah, I remember that," Lucas said.

"You do? You know Lord Savard then?" Louis asked, surprised.

"No, we just…we learned about it in school," Lucas answered.

Louis' eyes grew wide. "You are so fortunate to attend school," he said.

"Yeah, I guess we are," Lucas answered.

"Come, we will gather the tools we need and meet in the fields. We have much work ahead," Louis said.

They collected a few rakes and hoes, and then followed Pierre and Louis out to the fields. Lucas stopped suddenly when he looked out at the vast fields. "*That's* the garden?" he asked. Crops seemed to grow for miles in every direction, and people were already hard at work in the blazing sun.

"Yes, all this land belongs to the lord. Pierre's family is in charge of these strips of land. They must plow the land and sow the seeds. Then they tend the plants and harvest the crops," Louis explained.

"Wow. That's a lot of wheat!" Lucas said. "Do you plant anything else out there?"

"Yes, there are turnips, as well as other vegetables," Louis answered. "Now, we must get working before Lord Savard comes. He would be angry to see us at rest rather than at work."

Once in the fields, Pierre introduced Lucas, Marvin, and Nicole to his parents, who were glad to have extra help. Pierre's mother, who looked very pregnant, was bending over and weeding between rows of plants.

"Please. Let us do this. With all the extra people, you shouldn't have to work out here in the sun. Shouldn't you go and rest a little bit?" Lucas said to Pierre's mother. She just stared at him.

"She can't understand English," Nicole said. She repeated in French what Lucas had said. The woman smiled, but she still didn't seem to understand. Nicole spoke to her again in French, and the woman answered.

"What did she say?" Lucas asked.

"She said her back is sore and she hasn't had a rest in a fortnight, whatever that is. But she said she's not sure if she should do that. What if Lord Savard found her lazing about?" Nicole said. Pierre's father walked over to where they stood and asked what was happening. His wife explained to him. He nodded and said something to her, and she smiled and wiped her hands on her torn apron.

"*Merci*," she said to Lucas as she walked back toward the cottage. Pierre's father simply marched back into the fields.

"What was that all about?" Lucas asked.

"Pierre's dad said that with all the extra hands today, his wife could go inside and look after the house. She was happy to have the extra time," Nicole answered and turned to watch Pierre's mother enter the small cottage. Then Nicole turned back to Lucas, shielding her eyes from the sun. "By the way. You're a nice guy," she said. "But don't tell anyone I said that."

Lucas smiled. "Forget about it. I'm a *great* guy," he answered.

They spent most of the morning working in the fields. Pierre followed behind them, gathering the weeds they had pulled from the ground to feed the cow and pigs. At times, he disappeared into the barn to repair a broken tool or clean out the barn. He walked the cow outside to feed on grass and milked it. All the while, no one complained. Not about the hot sun, not about their blistering hands, not about their sore backs. Marvin was amazed at how much Pierre was able to do without his sight. He realized that Pierre did more things while completely blind than most people Marvin knew in modern times could do.

Pierre's mother brought more bread and water out to the group working in the fields, and they ate heartily. Marvin had never worked so hard in his life. His legs ached and his arms felt like rubber. By just past noon, he was so tired he was sure he was going to fall to the ground. Before he had a chance to complain, trumpets sounded off in the distance, grabbing his attention.

Everyone in the fields stood up and looked toward the center of the village. They started talking quietly to one another and quickly filed out of the fields toward the sound of the trumpets. Lucas, Marvin, and Nicole were too tired to ask what was happening. They followed everyone through the crops and past the small houses to the center of the village. Villages were built around the church, which stood at the center. As they walked toward the middle of the village they could see the steeple of the small church in the sky.

They arrived just in time to hear a well-dressed man begin shouting orders to the peasants. He was wearing a long, blue robe and a fancy, blue hat with a feather jutting out of the top of it. Marvin quickly realized that this was Lord Savard, the lord of the manor. He rode a muscular, brown horse that was draped in a blanket the same bright blue color as Lord Savard's robes. Four other men on horseback rode with him, two on either side.

"What's going on?" Lucas whispered to Nicole, who was trying hard to hear what Lord Savard had to say.

"I'm not sure. I think he's asking about who is planning to come and shear his sheep. He's telling them when they must provide him with payment after they take their crops to the market in town," she whispered. "Oh, now he's asking…"

"*Vous là! Que faîtes-vous là?*" Lord Savard shouted. He was looking in the direction of Louis, Lucas, Marvin, and Nicole. They looked at one another with worry.

I bet Lord Savard can read. What if he knows about King Charles' decree? Marvin thought.

Louis stepped forward to answer Lord Savard. After a brief conversation, Lord Savard gave Louis a dirty look, and he and his attendants left the village. People scattered in all directions, going back to their daily chores.

"What just happened, Louis? What did he say to you?" Marvin asked.

Louis looked concerned. "Nothing. He wanted to know what I was doing out here in the village with the peasants when I am a squire, especially one who wears the King's crest," he answered, distracted.

"Did he say anything about us being spies or anything?" Marvin asked.

Louis brushed his slightly long bangs out of his eyes. "No, but he said I should go back to the castle where I belong before I get into trouble."

No one asked another question of Louis. Instead of heading back to the fields, they followed him back to Pierre's barn. When they got to the front door of the barn, Louis looked over one shoulder, then the other. Marvin was sure that something was wrong, but Louis wasn't saying anything. He just opened the barn door and motioned for them all to follow him. Once inside, he sat down on a bale of hay and rested his elbows on his knees.

"I must go back. Something is not right. I can feel it. My king may need me, and I must go. He may have word from Sir Jean," he said.

"But what if you are in trouble? You looked worried. Those guys didn't seem very friendly to you," Marvin asked.

"It does not matter. I must go," Louis stated.

"Hey Louis, why are you so loyal to the King?" Lucas asked.

Louis drew a long breath and thought carefully for a moment. He looked each of them in the eye, and then looked down at the ground. "I was orphaned as a child. I only remember that I lived inside the palace dungeons all alone for a while. I was afraid. I used to sneak out of the castle using the trapdoor and come to this village," he said quietly. Pierre nodded his head.

"But you told us your father was a noble and taught you to speak English. That's what you said when we were here last time," Lucas said.

Louis hung his head low. "I lied to you. I could not explain how I knew your language. And I was ashamed that I had no family," he explained.

"Oh," Lucas mumbled.

Louis continued. "When I came to the village I met Pierre. We would play, and I would hide here, sneaking in and out of the castle to steal food for myself and for his family. Sir Jean the Fierce caught me near the castle, living as a thief. Instead of turning me in, he claimed that I was his nephew and asked the King if I could work in the castle as a page, doing chores. You must understand, this honor is only given to a child of a noble family. The King agreed, and he allowed me to apprentice with Sir Jean. I was taught to read and write, both in French and English. A few months ago, on my fourteenth birthday, I was asked to become a squire.

Now I will one day become an honored knight. I have had an opportunity that no peasant has ever had, and an orphan yet. They saved my life, Sir Jean and the King, and I owe them a debt of gratitude."

"Oh," Lucas said. "Um...I guess that's why you don't want to believe us about the King."

"*Oui*," Louis said.

"But Louis, if we are right, then the real king needs *you* this time. If there is an imposter, and he plans to kill King Charles VII tomorrow night, then you must help us," Marvin said.

Louis didn't say anything. He just stared at the ground.

"Listen, all you have to do is help us out a little bit. We aren't asking you to harm anyone, we just need to stop the imposter from hurting the King. We won't cause any trouble. If we get to the forest and we're wrong, we'll just go back to where we came from, and we'll never bother you again," Marvin said.

A flash of memory crossed Louis' face for a brief second. His eyes narrowed and then grew wide again. He looked out the small window in the barn wall. "Never again. Do not say that. I hope I will see you again," he said.

Something was very wrong with Louis. *Something is definitely going on*, Marvin thought.

"So then, what do you need from me?" Louis asked as he snapped out of his trance. "You must tell me what your plan is. I cannot promise to be part of it. I can only promise that I will do my best to keep you safe."

"We believe that the imposter is going to use the information he has gathered in our time to meet the real king in the forest as he returns from battle. That should take place tonight," Lucas said. "What we need to know is this: where is this forest by the river? The book we read says that the King returns 'through the royal forest, where the shallow bend allows travelers to ford the river.' Also, is the imposter king bringing any backup men with him?" Lucas grinned. "Oh, and one more thing. We also need a few weapons. Can you hook us up? I mean, can you get some for us?"

"I can give you blunted swords and dull-tipped lances. It is an offense to give an untrained swordsman a proper weapon. I will teach you to use them for defense only. And I will give you a shield. If you get into a fight, the shield will be the only thing to protect you," Louis answered.

Marvin bit his nails for a minute and thought about that. *How could we fight the imposter king? He is a trained swordsman and a real knight. Besides, the real king might be injured from battle and tired. We won't be able to defend the King ourselves, especially if Louis is the only one with a decent weapon.*

"We also need someone who knows the forest well and can fight Mr. LeClair," Lucas said. "Otherwise, he'll chop us to pieces."

"Who is Mr. LeClair?" Louis asked.

"He's our teacher. The imposter king," Lucas answered. "Okay, you're right. This sounds very unbelievable. But trust us, where we come from, he is a bad man who is up to no good."

"LeClair…LeClair…I know this name," Louis said thoughtfully.

"You might know his name. He is from King Charles' court, and he traveled through that wall in the dungeon to our time. He goes back and forth between times, gathering information from the future to use back here in 1450," Lucas explained.

"You are speaking of the swirling light, yes?" Louis said.

"Yes," Marvin said.

"And you insist that this light sends a person through time?" Louis asked.

"Well…we're here, aren't we?" Lucas said. "Anyway, we need someone who knows the forest."

"I do not know the forest well," Louis said. "The royal forest is the King's forest and is kept for his hunting only. Sometimes he allows his nobles to accompany him on a hunt. Otherwise, the forest is strictly forbidden. But I know someone who knows it well, and who has also been betrayed by the King. He would help you."

"Who?" Marvin asked. He already had an idea who it was.

"Jacques Coeur," Louis said. "But first, you would have to free him from the dungeons…if it is not too late already."

Lucas, Marvin, and Nicole looked at one another. Now they had to free Jacques from prison *and* make it to the forest on time to save the King. Not to mention the fact that they also had to go back through the portal at midnight. If they didn't go back tonight, after twenty-four hours, they might be trapped in medieval France. Things were getting more difficult by the minute.

Rescuing Jacques meant going back to the castle, and they were risking their lives just going back there. The King had a price on their heads, and every time they set foot in the castle they were in grave danger. Marvin sighed. They needed more help than they had, and Louis was not offering his full cooperation. Louis obviously felt torn about freeing a prisoner, no matter who it was, and he was hesitant about trespassing in the King's forest to fight a man that he did not completely believe was an imposter. Marvin knew all of this was hard for Louis, but they had only one choice. Louis was either in, or he was out.

"Louis, there is something else we will need," Marvin said.

"What is that?"

"You," Marvin answered.

8

Louis nodded his head thoughtfully, but he didn't answer. He stood up and looked out the window again. "I must go back to the castle," he announced. "I will return for you."

"Uh, Louis? Don't leave us here. We have to save the King—tonight. And then we have to get back through that wall at midnight," Lucas said.

"Oh, there is a time that this swirling light works then?" Louis asked.

"It goes like this. *Midnight fly, by twenty-four, back in time no time shall pass. Miss the door in twenty-four and no more,*" Lucas explained. "We have to use the portal at midnight and return home by the next night at midnight, or we can't go back at all."

Louis scrunched his eyebrows. "This is all very much for me to believe. But do not worry, I will return for you. As I have told you, I will make sure you are safe." He smiled shyly and glanced at Nicole. Then he said good-bye and left the barn.

"Well, back to the crops?" Lucas asked, standing up.

"*Non*, I have something else...you help me do," Pierre said in broken English. "It is past noon, *oui*? You have, how do you say, finish the work?"

"Oh, we've finished with the gardening?" Lucas said. "That's good news!"

"*Oui*, but...ahhh...*je dois entrer en ville*," Pierre tried to explain.

"You mean, you need to go into town?" Nicole translated.

"*Oui*. I load the wagon and sell it," he stumbled on his words. "If you come, *mon père* can stay and work."

"Well, if you need help loading the wagon and taking it into town, we would be happy to help you. I would love to see a medieval town," Marvin said. He thought it was a great idea. Pierre would need help going to town, and this way his father could stay behind and get more work done.

"Wait a minute. Pierre can't see. How will we find our way to the town?" Lucas asked. "Oh, no offense to Pierre."

Nicole rolled her eyes and translated to Pierre.

Pierre smiled. "That is fine. I understand. But you would be...um...surprised. I am able to do many things."

Lucas slapped him gently on the back. "I'm sure you can. Well, let's get going before Louis comes back for us."

"Yeah. Then we have to implement phase one of our plan," Marvin said. Phase one was supposed to include finding out when the fake king was leaving for the forest, and locating the royal forest and the bend in the river. But now, phase one was to free Jacques, the only person who knew the forest well enough to help them. He would also be the only skilled swordsman besides Louis on the mission. A definite asset. Especially since they had a plan to intercept Mr. LeClair, but no backup plan in case he fought back. And no one wanted to see Lucas wielding a sword.

Pierre led them out of the barn to a large wooden wagon. It had only two enormous, spoked wheels. The back of the wagon rested on the ground. They quickly loaded the wagon with baskets of fruit from the orchards, vegetables, and metal objects.

"What are these?" Lucas asked as he hoisted things into the wagon.

"Anvils, pots, horseshoes, and other iron stuff," Marvin answered. "They must have been made by a blacksmith."

Pierre smiled and nodded his head. He brought the horse around and harnessed it to the wagon. When the wagon was loaded, he lifted his arm high in the air, tilting his face to the sun.

"What is he doing?" Lucas whispered to Marvin and Nicole.

"I don't know. I think he might be trying to find north," Marvin answered. "That way he would be able to decide which direction we need to take."

"*Oui*. I will know the way," Pierre said. He grabbed the reins and finally led the horse off toward the left. "We go this way."

They followed Pierre and the horse all the way into town, stopping a few times so Pierre could double check that they were going in the right direction by asking Nicole questions about trees and nearby landmarks like ponds and streams. Marvin was amazed at how Pierre could find his way around. Pierre told them that his father always commented on the things around them on the way to town. Pierre knew what to "watch" for on the way to town, with the help of other people's eyes. Pierre explained that his brother tended one of the stalls in town and stayed there for a few days. Pierre and his father brought more goods to the market for his brother to sell so he didn't run out.

Marvin checked his glow watch. It was three o'clock. Still plenty of time to figure out what they were going to do—and when they would start their plan. He quickly took off the watch, thankful that Louis hadn't noticed it, and stuck it into the waistband of his tights, just like he did the last time they were in medieval France. Marvin chuckled to himself. It seemed so normal to say "just like last time we were in medieval France"—as if this was a normal family vacation or something. Except this was anything but normal.

Finally, they could hear the hustle and bustle of the town. As they approached the gates, Marvin's eyes grew wide. It wasn't a beautiful or magnificent city, but the buildings and the people were incredible. Wood and plaster buildings lined the streets. The second stories hung over the first stories, shading the dirt street below.

Before they entered the town, they passed a few men who collected coins from Pierre. "Do you have to pay to come in here?" Lucas asked.

"*Non*, you must pay…toll to bring goods. The land, it belongs to Lord Savard. The market toll…is to him," Pierre said.

They walked down a street that was crowded with people. As Marvin looked around, he could only think of one thing. The town smelled worse than the village! Garbage, rotten table scraps, and even animal dung littered the streets. He remembered learning that medieval folk threw all their garbage out their windows, but he had never thought about just how dirty that would be.

As they pushed through the busy street, Marvin noticed many different merchants selling their goods. A woman sitting at a large wooden loom shouted about her fine cloth. A man called out to them, trying to sell his sheep, which milled about in a small wooden pen. Two people stood beside what looked like an igloo made of straw. Bees buzzed noisily around the waist-high beehive, while the men called to passersby to buy the honey.

"Wow, look at his stuff," Lucas said, pointing to a well-dressed man in robes and a hat. He was standing in front of his stall, which was piled high with silks, spices, and jewelry. They all watched as the man shook hands with two other men and then pressed his fist into a blob of melted wax on a piece of paper. When he lifted his fist, his ring left a design in the wax.

Nicole spoke to Pierre, and he nodded. Pierre did not look, but he knew exactly who Nicole was talking about.

"He is *un commerçant*...a merchant...who comes from far. He should only come on merchant fair days, when other trades set up their stalls. But he travels, and comes often with...ah...things from far away," he said with a dirty look. "He pays high tolls. The lord allows him." Pierre obviously didn't like the stout, red-faced man.

Lucas tried to get a good look at the stuff the man had for sale and managed to catch a glimpse of his ring. "That's his mark cut into the ring, right?" Lucas asked. He moved closer to try to see what design was cut into the top of the silver ring.

"*Oui.* Each person...has their own mark," Pierre said.

"Like a coat of arms?" Marvin asked.

"*Oui, exactement,*" Pierre answered.

The merchant looked at the group twice as they passed. He seemed to be looking carefully at their clothes. The two men he was talking to wore a coat of arms on their tunics, and they each held a scroll of parchment paper in their hands. They looked closely at Lucas, Nicole, Marvin, and Pierre as they passed by, glancing down at the papers they were holding.

Lucas nudged Marvin and nodded his head toward the men. "I wonder what's so interesting on that paper," he whispered. "I hope it's not the King's decree about us being spies!"

Marvin quickly looked over at the men with the scrolls. He couldn't see what was on the paper, but the men were certainly acting suspiciously. Marvin began to feel worried. That scroll could mean that the King's decree had reached the town. If so, they were in for some trouble. He looked away and locked eyes with Lucas. Lucas looked like he was thinking the same thing. They had to find out what was on that scroll. If the word was out, they would have to leave town immediately!

Up ahead, Marvin could see a young boy who looked around sixteen years old. He also looked exactly like Pierre. When the boy saw Pierre, he shouted and waved.

Pierre heard his voice and led the wagon to his brother's stall. "*Bonjour,* Claude!"

"*Ah, bonjour!*" his brother said, giving Pierre a hug. "*Comment ça va?*"

"*Ça va bien, merci, et vous?*" Lucas, Marvin, and Nicole said in unison. It was an automatic response. In school, whenever the French teacher asked the class how they were, they replied "*Ça va bien, merci, et vous?*"

Pierre and his brother stared at them for a moment. Nicole giggled.

"*Bien!*" Claude answered. "*Qui est là?*"

Pierre answered Claude in French, and Nicole translated to Marvin and Lucas.

"Pierre told his brother that we're friends of Louis, but that we would be leaving tonight," Nicole told them.

Claude's face turned serious and he said something else to Pierre.

"Now what did he say?" Lucas asked, concerned by the look on Claude's face.

"He warned Pierre to be careful of strangers, especially since we're friends of Louis. He said to remember that Louis is from a strange country, no matter where he lives now," Nicole told them.

"What does he mean, that he's from a strange country?" Lucas asked. "Where is he from?"

Marvin shrugged his shoulders.

Pierre introduced everyone. Claude then went about unloading the cart and filling his stall. Lucas, Pierre, Nicole, and Marvin helped him, and in no time the wagon was empty.

Claude didn't speak to them very much. Marvin figured it was partly because he didn't know much English and partly because he didn't trust them, being friends of Louis. On the way back to the village, Marvin asked Pierre about it.

"Pierre, your brother doesn't seem to like Louis very much. I thought you have known each other since you were children," Marvin said.

"This is true. But *mon frère*...he is older...and Louis was a young thief...with...how do you say...no parents," Pierre said.

"So your brother didn't like him because he was an orphan?" Marvin asked.

"*Non*, he remembers...Louis came to the village as a young boy...he spoke not French...he had different ideas." Pierre tried to explain the best he could. "My brother thinks always there is...uh... something different with Louis."

Marvin nodded his head. "But you are good friends with Louis?"

Pierre smiled. "He is like a brother to me. He helps *ma famille*. He brings us things from the castle. He brings food. Sometimes he earns money. He gives it to us."

"Wow. What a nice guy," Lucas said. "I could use a friend like that."

Nicole reached over and slapped him on the arm. Lucas looked offended.

On the way back to the village, Marvin saw the men with the scroll talking to other merchants. Then he noticed the paper lying on the ground at their feet. Marvin had a funny feeling about that piece of paper. He was worried that the men were warning the villagers of the spies and of the King's reward of thirty gold coins. If that were true, then Lucas, Marvin, and Nicole had to run. Fast.

He looked over at Lucas and knew his friend was thinking the same thing. Lucas winked at Marvin and then motioned to Nicole.

"*Psst.* Hey, Nicole. Go over there and ask those men how much the chickens cost," Lucas whispered.

Nicole looked at Lucas like he had three heads. "What?"

"Just do it. I need you to distract them for a minute, and you speak French better than Marvin," he said. Nicole just stood there. "Just trust me, will you?" he whispered.

Nicole took a deep breath and walked over to the men Lucas had pointed out. She began speaking French. Lucas crept up quietly behind her, keeping low to the ground. When they were all looking over at Nicole, Lucas reached out and snatched the scroll that had fallen to the ground. Then he snuck away.

Nicole walked over shortly afterward. "Okay, why did you just make me do that?" she asked.

Lucas did not say a word. He handed Nicole the scroll.

Marvin peered over her shoulder and tried to read what was written on the scroll. As he read the scroll, he started hoping that his French abilities were worse than he thought.

When Nicole gasped, Marvin knew he had read the document correctly.

Now Marvin was really worried. They had to find Louis as quickly as possible. His whole life depended on it.

The letter was addressed to the Scots Archers, and to a group of German soldiers that the letter said were "on hire" to the King of France. Nicole read it out loud in English. "His Majesty, King Charles VII, does hereby decree that anyone wearing the crest bearing His Majesty's coat of arms is to be captured for execution. On order of the King this day, August 12, 1450." The decree was sealed with wax at the bottom.

The three friends studied the paper and then looked at each other. Louis was in trouble. He was wearing the crest with the King's coat of arms.

"We have to find Louis, fast!" Marvin said. He was sick to his stomach with the thought of Louis being caught. He had quickly become a good friend, not to mention a handy tour guide.

They quickly explained the situation to Pierre. Then they all rushed back to the village, hoping with every step that Louis would make it back, too, and that he hadn't been caught at the castle.

So many things went through Marvin's mind. If Louis were caught, he would be locked away and executed. Marvin grew more and more worried every second. Then he realized something else. If Louis were caught, he wouldn't be able to come to find them, and they would never find the castle alone. They might never get to stop Mr. LeClair.

Now the imposter king had two plots: one against the real King and another against supporters of the King.

When they got back to the village, they hurried into Pierre's barn to wait for Louis. Time seemed to tick by slowly as they waited for him to come through the barn door. Marvin continued to worry about their friend.

Lucas stood up. "We have to go and help him," he said.

"How? We don't even know how to find him. We don't know where they would be keeping him," Marvin said.

"Pierre. He can lead us there, right, Pierre?" Lucas answered.

Just then Louis burst into the barn, panting. He ran to the window and scanned the countryside, watching to see if anyone had followed him. After a few moments, he turned around.

"We were just talking about you," Lucas said. "Are you okay?"

Louis paced the floor. "Something is wrong. I went back to the castle, and the guards immediately tried to seize me. I told them I was the squire of Sir Jean the Fierce, but they did not release me. I broke free and ran. I do not understand," he said, running his hand through his wavy hair.

Marvin stepped forward and handed Louis the paper. "I think you should read this," he said.

Louis' face grew more and more red as he read the King's decree.

"Louis, remember those knights and squires visiting from Germany who you jousted with when we were here during our last visit? Where are they now?" Marvin asked. Suddenly, he was piecing it all together.

"They are still here. They have been hired by the King to stay on at the castle while many of our knights are away at battle. That is why they were invited to take part in the joust. They are here to help us," Louis answered.

"No, they are here to harm you," Marvin said. "That letter is also addressed to them. That's why the squire you jousted with changed his lance at the last moment. That's why he wanted to switch the dull lance for the sharp, poison-tipped one. He must have been hired to get rid of you. Only he failed, thanks to Jacques. They didn't succeed at the joust, so they marked you. The crest that you wear—it's a target. You weren't given the crest as a badge of honor. You were given it as a mark of death.

"Now, the King's guards and the hired knights from Germany are looking for you. The King has ordered that they capture anyone wearing the crest. Then he can blame your death on the knights from Germany. He will convince the illiterate peasants and villagers that the German knights acted on their own, and he will not be blamed. No one would even know," Marvin said. "The joust was supposed to be a way to get rid of you. And the squire you battled was hired by the King himself."

"But where did this letter come from?" Louis asked, confused.

"I saw that man—the rich merchant—in town giving a rolled-up piece of paper to those other men he was talking to. The soldiers. In fact, the merchant set his seal in the wax," Lucas said.

"Yes, but the two men had patches on their shirts with a coat of arms, too. It looked just like the one Louis wears," Nicole said.

"Ah, but you are wrong, milady," Lucas said. "The coat of arms on the men's tunics was embroidered in different-colored thread. And the words were different."

"Really? Wow, good eye," Nicole said.

Lucas smiled proudly. "You know what else? They were checking us out pretty closely. It's a good thing Louis wasn't with us at the time. They seemed to be looking for a specific crest. *Your* crest," Lucas added.

Louis didn't move for a few moments. He did not say a word. His face was stone serious. Suddenly, he reached up to the chest of his tunic and tore the crest from the fabric. He held the crest in his clenched fist as he spoke through gritted teeth. "I have been betrayed by my King," he said. He threw the crest to the floor.

"No, you have been betrayed by an imposter," Marvin corrected.

Lucas bent down to pick up the crest that lay on the dirty ground. He studied it closely. That small crest had huge meaning. All along, Louis had thought it was something special. In reality, it was a mark of shame.

Louis started taking deep breaths and pacing the barn. His eyes blazed with fury. "I cannot believe this. I cannot believe it is I who is hunted," he panted.

"Don't worry, Louis. We'll help you. Just like you promised us, we'll do everything we can to make sure you are safe," Lucas said. "But now you must believe us about the imposter, right?"

Louis sighed and nodded his head. "*Oui*, what you have said must be true."

"Now, let's sit down and figure out what we can do tonight, before we go back," Marvin said.

They all sat down in a circle in the barn. Pierre went outside to tend to the cow and the other animals. The four of them went over every detail of the plan.

First, they had to free Jacques so he could help them through the King's forest and fight Mr. LeClair. Jacques would certainly believe them, if he was still alive. Before locking him up, the King had said that Jacques knew too much. Marvin figured that Jacques must have suspected that the King was really an imposter.

Besides, freeing Jacques was the right thing to do, since he had helped Louis during the joust. So, they had to get into the castle, free Jacques, get to the forest, and save the King—all before midnight.

The last part of the plan was more difficult. How could they overcome an imposter who is a skilled swordsman? Louis had agreed to arm them with weapons for self-defense, but they wouldn't have any real weapons. They could rely on Jacques and Louis, but what if they couldn't take Mr. LeClair alone?

"I could back them up. I know karate," Lucas said. Nicole started laughing.

"What?" he asked.

"Lucas, you were what, five years old? You only took karate for a few months, and you said you didn't like the hitting or kicking. What will you do, slap the guy to death?" Nicole said through fits of laughter.

"Oh. Nice. See, that's the problem with being friends with someone almost your whole life. They know your 'stuff' and they use it against you. Come on. I learned some fighting strategies," he said. He raised his fists to chest level.

"Yeah. Okay. Whatever," she said. Then she used her fake sweet voice. "Yes, you are so tough you could take on any knight, Lucas Maxwell. And may the force be with you."

"Uh, that's from *Star Wars*, not the medieval times of knights. Nice try, though," he answered.

"Can you guys stop it for just a day?" Marvin sighed. "Seriously, what do we do if Jacques and Louis can't take Mr. LeClair alone?"

"We could throw things at him. Drop something on him. Circle him and trip his horse… um…" Lucas said. They all stared at him. "Hey, this is called brainstorming, people. We just throw ideas out there, good or bad, to get the ideas flowing until a good one pops up. That's what Mrs. Lindsay says. Doesn't anyone else pay attention in class, or what?"

"Oh brother, he's quoting his English teacher again. You just like her because she coaches basketball," Nicole said.

Lucas thought his homeroom teacher, Mrs. Wright, was awesome, but he thought Mrs. Lindsay was amazing, too. She was tall and fit, with long, sandy colored hair and a great laugh. She taught English and reading, coached many teams, and even taught music. Lucas looked forward to school every day because of her.

"Hey, who says I like her? Anyway, she has great ideas, so come on. Get brainstorming," he said, blushing a little.

They came up with all kinds of ideas, like surprising Mr. LeClair in the bushes, lassoing him with a rope, and scaring him with masks. All their ideas seemed silly.

"What if we send Jacques out first, and then we distract Mr. LeClair so that Jacques can knock him off his horse?" Lucas said.

"Hm. Not bad," Nicole said. "How do we distract him?"

"I don't know. Act weird. Do gymnastics. Run screaming from the bushes." Lucas kept throwing ideas out there.

"I've got it!" Marvin said. "All I need is to get back into the castle dungeons."

"What a coincidence. We happen to be going there tonight!" Lucas said. "Speaking of the castle, we'd better head back there and make sure we can still get in with all the security. Then we need to find Mr. LeClair. We have some spying to do."

By the time they said good-bye to Pierre and left the village, it was six o'clock. The sun was still blazing in the sky, but they knew that by the time they got to the castle it would be evening.

They walked the long path through the field, keeping an eye out for anyone coming in pursuit. It was quiet, except for the sound of birds. When they reached the hill, they could see the castle up ahead.

They crept up the hill slowly and quietly, listening for any movement other than their own. Finally, they arrived at the grove of trees outside the moat.

Louis scanned the castle, looking for any signs of guards on the walls or in the windows.

"I wish you had your binoculars," Lucas whispered to Marvin.

"Except they weren't invented until 1608. That would be a problem. It's important that we don't bring inventions back in time. It could mess things up totally," Marvin answered. Then he thought of the watch he was carrying in the waistband of his pants. He felt guilty bringing it along, but after all, they would need it. How else would they make it back to the portal on time?

There didn't seem to be any unusual activity, so Louis motioned for them to walk toward the drawbridge.

"Aren't we taking the usual way in?" Marvin asked. He expected them to use the long plank over the thick, stinky moat.

"*Non*, it is not dark outside. Someone would see us for sure. We will join a group of people entering the gates. Try to blend in and do not look the guards in the eye," Louis explained.

They walked quickly until they were close behind a group of people entering the castle gate. The guards did their usual scan of the crowd. Marvin was nervous. He hoped no one would stop them. Within seconds they were across the bridge and through the gate. Louis peered out into the courtyard to make sure that guards weren't swarming the area. When Louis gave them the signal, they stepped into the courtyard and looked around.

"We need to get to the trapdoor without anyone seeing us. This is more difficult with four people. If anyone sees you, you must stop immediately and wait for a better moment," Louis said quietly, his worried eyes scanning the buildings around the courtyard.

Marvin checked his watch. It was seven-thirty. The sun was getting low in the sky, and a rosy glow lit up the courtyard enough to help them find their way around.

They walked casually toward the castle, its colorful flags rippling in the gentle wind. People passed them by but paid them no attention, which Marvin thought was a good sign. At least there wasn't an "all points bulletin" out for their arrest. The King's decree about the spies hadn't put them in too much trouble, and Louis was not wearing the mark anymore. *Maybe we'll make it inside without a hitch*, Marvin thought. Not a moment later, he heard the thunderous pounding of horses' hooves. A group of armed guards stormed into the courtyard.

"Arrêtez au nom du roi!" one of them shouted. Then the other guard shouted something else.

"They are looking for anyone who wears the crest!" Nicole whispered.

The four guards, all mounted on horseback, were dressed in full armor, but their helmets left their unshaven faces fully visible. They looked dirty and mean, and they meant business. They stopped to speak to a few people in the courtyard before their eyes fell on Lucas, Marvin, Nicole, and Louis. Suddenly, they started to come toward them.

One of the guards shouted again, his voice loud and commanding. Nicole turned pale. "They're looking for you, Louis! They know about the crest!" she said, horrified.

Louis froze. He looked at Marvin, Nicole, and Lucas. No one knew what to do.

"If they catch Louis, we're doomed," Nicole whispered. "Or they'll take us all."

Lucas reached into his pocket and leaned over and spoke in Marvin's ear. "Get those two out of here and meet me at the arrow loop," he said in a low voice.

Marvin frowned at Lucas.

"Just trust me," Lucas said, and he gave Marvin a gentle shove.

Marvin put his arms around Nicole and Louis' shoulders. He started slowly pushing them on, keeping an eye on Lucas the whole time. They were only a few steps away when Lucas suddenly held up the crest and walked up to the guards. "I am the one who wears the crest," he said.

⇒10⇐

The guards leaped into action and grabbed Lucas by the arms.

"N—" Louis started to shout.

Marvin clapped a hand over Louis' mouth before he could get the word out. Nicole started to run toward the guards, but Marvin quickly grabbed her wrist and pulled her back.

"It's too late! Don't let them get us, too!" he whispered. Louis struggled under his hand. "If we get caught, it will just make things worse. Louis, we need you more than ever now." He held onto Louis until he was sure that the guards weren't paying any attention to them.

Marvin felt terrible watching his best friend get dragged away by the guards. He had no idea that Lucas was planning to give himself up as the decoy. But there was nothing they could do now. Marvin figured that Lucas had a plan. He would talk his way out of it. He would be released just as soon as Louis and the others were out of danger. He would convince the guards that he was just some dumb kid from far away. Any minute, Lucas would go free. Marvin was sure of it. Still, his hands grew sweatier by the second as he watched Lucas being dragged away.

The guards led Lucas through the courtyard, holding firmly to each arm. Two others followed behind on their horses, swords ready for action. Lucas seemed to be looking around for his friends. The guards were talking loudly in French, and then they started laughing.

Nicole's face turned completely white.

"What, Nicole? What did they say?" Marvin asked anxiously.

"They said the prisoners will be beheaded tonight at eight o'clock in the public square," she whimpered. "Including Lucas."

"No! This is not right. It is me they are looking for. Not him," Louis said. He tried to push past Nicole and Marvin.

Marvin stopped him. "Louis, don't! We need you. If we are going to save Jacques and the King, then we need you—alive! We have a few hours. We will just have to rescue Jacques *and* Lucas."

Louis shook his head sadly. "I have put you all in terrible danger," he said.

"We put *ourselves* in danger, Louis. We aren't even supposed to be here," Nicole assured him.

"Neither am I," he answered quietly.

"What do you mean? Just because you were an orphan doesn't mean you can't become a knight in the King's castle. You belong here as much as anyone else," Nicole said.

"No, that is not it. When I saw you come through the wall, I realized something," Louis said.

"What?" Nicole asked.

"I realized that I had seen that before. I had *done* that before," he said quietly.

"Wh…what do you mean?" Marvin asked.

"All this time, I thought I was an orphan. I don't remember my parents. I only remember that I woke up one day lying on the ground in the King's dungeon. I was a small child. I hid for a while, and finally found a way to sneak out. That's when I found my way to the village. It was later that Sir Jean the Fierce found me and took me on as a squire," he answered.

"So…where are you from?" Marvin asked.

"I don't know. I was only five years old. But when I saw you come through the wall…" his voice trailed off and he gazed out across the courtyard.

"What? You felt something?" Nicole asked.

"I felt that I remembered that wall…and the swirling light. And a flood of memories came back. My parents. A forest. A cave. A coin. I fear I may not belong here, either," he said.

Nicole's mouth dropped open. "No way! You think you might have come through the wall, too?" Then she made a squeaky sound. "Wait, you…you remember a cave and a forest?" She looked at Marvin in disbelief.

"*Oui,*" Louis said quietly.

Marvin and Nicole stared at him. "So you are the kid from the legend," Marvin whispered. He couldn't believe it. The legend of the ghost of Green Hills, the one Grandpa Dave had told him ever since he was a kid, was true. Marvin remembered that legend almost word for word. "*Hundreds of years ago, there was a family living in these woods. They discovered a cave. The parents let their young son play in it every day while they hunted. One day, they walked in just in time to see their son vanish. He simply walked into the wall and disappeared into thin air. His parents never saw him again.*"

Poor Louis, Marvin thought. *He was just a kid when he vanished into the wall.*

But one thing did not make sense. If Louis had traveled through the wall, he shouldn't be alive. *Miss the door in twenty-four and no more*, Marvin repeated in his head. *I thought that meant you were "no more." I thought that meant you would not exist anymore. And clearly, he exists.*

"This is…this is so…" Nicole said.

"Unbelievable? We're here, aren't we?" Marvin said. Although he was eager to solve this mystery of Louis', he knew it had to wait. They had only half an hour before the public beheading. They had to go out into the courtyard to the chopping block. They had to find Jacques and Lucas, and keep out of sight of the imposter king.

"Louis, we'll try to help you. But first, we have to save Lucas and Jacques," Marvin said.

Louis nodded. "All right. Let us do what must be done."

People were filing into the courtyard from many different doorways. They all moved in the same direction and were talking about the beheading. Marvin, Nicole, and Louis followed quietly behind them, keeping their heads down so as not to be noticed.

At the other end of the courtyard, a grand stage was set with a throne and a few smaller chairs on either side. A table sat in front of the throne and held a gold chalice. The King took his seat on the throne. He took a sip from the chalice and placed it back on the table. His green eyes danced with amusement at the sight of the chopping block being set up.

Nicole covered her eyes. "I can't watch this," she whined.

"Well, we can't let them lop off their heads anyway, so you can uncover your eyes," Marvin said. "You need to get a grip on yourself. We only have a few minutes left to get them out of there. Come on!"

Nicole and Louis followed him through the crowd toward the stage. Marvin looked at the stage.

The equipment was being readied. The prisoners were nowhere in sight.

"Where are they being kept?" Marvin asked.

"The dungeons," Louis said.

"Okay. Let's go," Marvin whispered.

"Wait. We cannot take the trapdoor leading down to the dungeons. Someone might see us," Louis said.

Marvin looked around frantically at all the doors leading into the castle. They were all carefully guarded. "Well, there's no other way in. Even if we do manage to get past the doors, it wouldn't be quick enough. We have to use the trapdoor."

"*D'accord*," Louis said. "Follow me."

They crept toward the trapdoor, watching the people around them to make sure no one was watching. It seemed that all eyes were on the stage for the beheading. Just as they were about to lift the hatch, two guards walked by. Marvin, Louis, and Nicole stood up and pretended to be doing nothing. The guards were talking in French. Louis' face grew more worried.

"Well? What did they say?" Marvin asked impatiently.

"They said that the prisoners have been taken to the execution," he answered.

Marvin searched the crowd for any sign of Lucas and the other prisoners. He looked up at the platform, but no one was there yet. "Well, where are they?" Marvin said. "Louis, what happens to the prisoners when they are taken out of their cells and led to the execution out here?"

"The prisoners are given a meal and their last rites. Then they are led from the dungeons by cart to the platform. Sometimes, if the guards think there is a chance that someone might set the prisoners free, they are taken to a secret room first and then are led here," Louis answered.

Marvin looked around one more time. There was no sign of a cart. "Where is the secret room?" he asked impatiently.

Louis shook his head in disappointment. "I do not know," he said.

Marvin looked along the walls of the castle. Every window looked the same. How would he find the secret room? He looked at his watch. Ten minutes until the beheading. They needed help, fast. They needed some kind of sign.

Suddenly, a glint of light caught Marvin's eye. Up in one of the windows, a few stories above the platform where the beheading would take place, a light glinted into the courtyard. At first, Marvin thought it was the sun reflecting on stained glass. Then he noticed a pattern. The light went on and off, sometimes in long blinks, sometimes in short ones. He focused on the window and realized that the blinking light was telling him something. It was Morse code. Marvin looked around the courtyard in disbelief. No one else seemed to be paying attention to the light.

Marvin was stunned. *It must be Lucas*, he thought. *I didn't know he knew Morse code.* He concentrated hard on the blinking lights. Three short blinks followed by three long blinks, and then three short ones again. S.O.S.! Marvin watched carefully as more blinks followed the first message. He nodded his head and turned to Louis and Nicole. "I've got it!" he said. "Follow me!"

"What are you talking about? We need to wait out here. They'll be here any minute," Nicole said.

"No, I know where they are. Lucas just told me," Marvin tried to explain.

Nicole looked at him, concerned. "Marvin... what do you mean he just told you? He isn't here. Are you okay?"

Marvin smirked. "Trust me. He told me where he is," he said. "Louis, take us to the chapel."

When no one was looking, Louis held the trapdoor open slightly. Marvin crouched down and held onto the sides of the opening. Then he dropped to the ground and quickly moved out of the way. Nicole fell into the basement soon after. They both dusted the dirt off their clothes as they stood up, waiting for Louis. Louis had insisted on going last. He said there was a chance that the last person to go through the opening in the ground would be caught.

They looked up at the trapdoor. It was closed. After a few seconds, Marvin started to worry. "Oh no," he said. "If they got Louis, we're doomed. I have no idea how to get to the chapel, and it would take more than just the two of us to rescue those three." He bit his nails anxiously.

Marvin was so busy worrying about how they would make it to the chapel that he didn't see the thin crack of light form above him. The trapdoor was opening. A few seconds later, Louis' feet and legs lowered down into the cellar. Then he dropped to the ground and landed on his feet. The trapdoor fell shut with a *thump*.

Marvin sighed. "There you are. I was starting to get worried."

"I had to wait for some guards to pass," Louis said. He looked around the dungeons and held up his hand as if to say "wait a minute." He listened intently to the sounds of the dungeon, and then, satisfied that there weren't any other guards around at the moment, he put down his hand and motioned for them to follow him.

They walked quietly through the damp, cool darkness until they got to the set of stairs leading up. Before they started up the stairs, Marvin remembered what he needed from the dungeons.

"Wait! Louis, where did you hide our clothes?" he asked.

Louis looked at him with a strange expression on his face. "They were at the end of this hall, buried near the prisoners' cells. Why do you need them now?" he asked.

"I don't need my clothes. I need something else," Marvin called back over his shoulder as he took off down the dingy corridor. He passed the small hallway to the left where the portal was located. Straight ahead of him were the prisoners' cells and a chair. There was a lump near the chair, covered in straw.

Marvin darted for the pile and pulled out his knapsack. He had put a few things in that bag before he left home, just in case. Now, these were the items he needed for the final confrontation in the forest. Also hidden in the pile were their clothes that they had left behind on their first trip to the castle. *Oh yeah! I can get my flashlight back now!* Marvin thought. He searched frantically for his shorts. Finally, he found them. Relieved, he held them up to retrieve his flashlight. His face fell in disappointment. The small blue flashlight was not clipped onto his belt loop. He fumbled with the other clothes in the pile, and he searched the ground around him. It was nowhere to be found.

"Pssst!" he heard coming from down the hall. Time was running out.

Marvin checked the ground one more time. *The flashlight must have fallen off sometime after we landed in the dungeon last time,* he figured.

He ran down the hallway to the stairs where Louis and Nicole stood waiting. Nicole threw her hands up in frustration and gave him an angry look. "Let's get going already," she said quietly. "Lucas' and Jacques' lives are depending on us!"

"Okay. But how are we going to get them out of the chapel?" Marvin asked. "Is there any other way out of there?"

"*Oui*, there is one trapdoor, beneath the altar," Louis explained.

"Boy, you guys sure have a lot of trapdoors around here. Are you positive?" Marvin asked.

"We have many trapdoors and secret passageways, some of which have never even been used. I know of most of them because I have used them. The trapdoor in the chapel allows the priest to escape in case of an attack," Louis answered.

"Where does it lead to?" Marvin asked.

"To the landing on the first floor, near the door," Louis answered. "Why?"

"Okay. Here's the plan. We need to get inside that room to get them out. Who would they let inside?" Marvin asked.

"I do not know. No one would be allowed to see the prisoners. The guards would be armed," Louis said.

"But you told me that they sometimes get their last meal and receive their final rites, right?" Marvin asked impatiently.

"*Oui*, that is true," Louis answered. "So we can send someone in with food. That would have to be Nicole, since they would send in a woman from the kitchen. But I am the only one who knows how to use the trapdoor. They will not believe that I was the one asked to bring the food to the prisoners."

Marvin was thinking. Then he smiled and nodded his head. "We need a priest's robe and a tray with water."

Nicole stared at him. "Have you gone mad?" she asked.

Marvin sighed. "Nicole, I'm serious. Since we can't go in and fight the guards, we need a decoy. You go in and tell the guards that you have been ordered to bring the last meal to the prisoners before they are executed. Louis, you go with her and say you are the priest. If you have a robe on, they should let you in. Tell them you need a few quiet moments with the prisoners and ask the guards to wait outside the door. Then, get the prisoners out through the trapdoor. I'll meet you on the landing on the first floor."

"How are we supposed to find a robe and a tray with water right now?" Nicole asked.

"We can get it from the kitchen. It is only up the stairs. Wait here," Louis said. He hurried up the stairs and came back within a minute. "I have a tray, a pitcher for water, and a loaf of bread. I also found this." He held a black hooded cape in his hands. It didn't look exactly like a priest's robe, but it would have to do.

"What if the guards won't leave the room?" Nicole asked.

"Then we're all going to the chopping block," Marvin said. "You have to convince them that you are bringing in a holy man to give the prisoners their last rites and their final meal."

They walked up the circular stairs with their backs against the wall. There would be a guard near the exit door, which was by the landing on the ground level. They climbed the stairs to ground level with Louis leading the way. He stopped when he got to the landing and slowly peeked around the corner to make certain the guard was not looking. Then he quickly moved across the landing and continued up the next flight of circular stairs. Nicole went next, pausing to check for the guard, and then darting up the second set of stairs. Marvin followed behind. As he passed the landing, he heard the guard say something.

Marvin stopped in his tracks, trying to think of an excuse as to why he was in the stairway. He didn't know if he should run or make up a lie.

Then Marvin heard another voice. The guard laughed and called out something else. Marvin relaxed. The guard hadn't been talking to him after all. He continued up the flight of stairs, past the second floor.

Finally, Marvin could see a door open at the next landing just ahead of him. Louis and Nicole were waiting at the doorway. *The chapel must be on the third floor*, Marvin thought.

Marvin quickly caught up to them. "I'll wait to make sure you get into the chapel, then I'll meet you on the landing in the stairwell on the first floor," he whispered. Louis put on the cape, and Nicole held out the tray. They nodded, turned left, and walked down the torch-lit hallway while Marvin watched from behind the door.

The chapel was on the left-hand side. Marvin recognized the hallway. They had been given a tour of the castle before and had seen the chapel. This time, however, it wouldn't be a pleasure trip.

Nicole looked back at Marvin nervously as she and Louis inched toward the chapel door. Then she straightened up, took a deep breath, and knocked loudly.

Back on the landing, Marvin pulled the door shut, leaving just a crack for him to peer through.

The guard who answered the door was not wearing armor, but wore a red cloak with a coat of arms emblazoned with "Scots Archers." It was their ceremonial costume. The guards obviously did not expect a daring rescue attempt, even though the prisoners were taken to the secret room.

Marvin crossed his fingers. He could not hear what was being said, but he could see what was happening. The guard summoned the other guards to the door. Marvin began to worry that they did not believe Louis and Nicole. A moment later, however, the three guards exited the room, and Nicole and Louis entered. The door creaked closed behind them. *Thank you, thank you, thank you,* Marvin chanted quietly to himself.

He turned quietly, closed the hall door, and started down the spiral stone stairway. When he got to the door on the first floor, Nicole and Louis emerged from a small opening near the floor. They pushed aside a large, square stone and wriggled free. Lucas, Jacques, and two other hooded men followed behind them.

"Am I glad to see you!" Lucas said as he passed Marvin.

When Marvin looked over toward the slightly open door leading to the courtyard outside, he could see the arm of a guard.

"Allow me," Lucas whispered. He ran in tackle mode toward the door and burst the door wide open, hitting the guard. The guard went down like a sack of potatoes from the surprise attack.

"That's one way to get past a guard," Marvin called. He followed Lucas out the doorway, with Nicole, Louis, Jacques, and the two other prisoners close behind.

The people in the courtyard were still anxiously awaiting the arrival of the prisoners, and had no idea yet that the prisoners were already in their midst.

Lucas turned back and smiled. Quickly, he spotted a horse and cart loaded with hay and a crate of chickens. He ran up to the man holding the reins and tapped him on the shoulder.

"In the name of the King, I must commandeer your vehicle," he boomed in his deepest voice.

"*Quoi?*" the man asked.

"Just give me that," he said to the man. He motioned to Louis to get on the horse. The man began shouting at them in French. Luckily, the trumpeters were announcing the beginning of the execution proceedings. No one paid any attention to the enraged man.

Lucas ran around to the back of the cart and climbed aboard. Then he opened the chicken crate. "Fly. Be free," he said. The chickens clucked out slowly, and Lucas held out his hand to pull Marvin, Nicole, and Jacques into the cart. The two other prisoners fled through the crowd. When the cargo was safely loaded, Louis kicked the horse and snapped the reins. The horse and cart took off through the courtyard toward the main gate. The King was giving a speech as the crowd cheered. Marvin knew that any minute, the imposter king would realize that the prisoners were late. Then he would find out that the prisoners were gone. Then there would be trouble.

The cart sped through the arched entranceway toward the drawbridge, which was still open. The guards at the drawbridge did not even try to stop the exiting cart, since they had no warning that the prisoners had escaped.

Marvin held onto the wooden rail around the cart. He watched the castle grow smaller and smaller as the cart bumped and rattled down the hill and through the fields.

Although they could hear the din of voices in the distance, no one was coming after them. Marvin figured they had made it over the drawbridge in the nick of time. Once the King realized that the prisoners had escaped, he would have secured the castle and there would have been no way out. Now, there was no way in.

They galloped through the countryside as the last glow of the sun disappeared behind the horizon. They had to slow down as it got darker.

Louis held the reins like a skilled horseman, checking over his shoulder regularly to make sure he hadn't lost anyone.

When Marvin was pretty certain that no one was coming after them, he turned around to face the group. Nicole was talking in French to Jacques, who looked both shocked and relieved. Lucas was sitting in a pile of hay with a piece of straw between his teeth.

"I can't believe you did that!" Marvin said.

"Did what?" Lucas asked nonchalantly.

"You know. Tackled the guard, stole a horse and cart, and got us out of there," Marvin said, laughing. "I mean, no offense, but you're not always known for thinking on your feet."

Lucas sat up straight. "Hmm. Should I take that as a compliment or an insult?" He rubbed his chin and looked up into the darkened sky. "What the heck. I pick compliment. And thanks. I can be awesome when I want to be."

Nicole joined the conversation. "Yeah, Lucas. Way to go! I can't believe we got out of there like that. It was like a scene from a movie…only instead of whooping and hollering from the cart, I was about to be sick. I thought we were goners."

"I know what you mean. I didn't see a way out of there," Marvin said, shaking his head.

"Ah shucks, twern't nothin'," Lucas drawled in a Texan accent. He tipped his imaginary hat toward Nicole. She laughed and shook her head.

Lucas rubbed his neck. "Hey, you guys found us in the nick of time, huh? My neck hurt just thinking about that chopping block."

"Well, good idea sending me the message about where to find you. I didn't get it at first, until I realized it was Morse code. Brilliant!" Marvin said.

"What message?" Lucas asked. He was examining the skin on his arms where the rope had cut into his wrists.

"You know, the light you flashed me in Morse code about how to find you. What did you use to send the signal?" Marvin asked.

"It wasn't me," Lucas said, rubbing his wrist. "Man, that kills."

"What are you talking about? You sent me a message by Morse code. S.O.S. Chapel. Three guards. Don't you remember? You gave me the S.O.S.," Marvin insisted.

Lucas stared at him. "Dude, I didn't give you any message. I don't even know Morse code. I wish I would have thought of that to save my own neck, but I was too busy whimpering like a baby."

"But…I saw it…" Marvin stammered.

"Uh, no. You saw the sun glinting off a piece of metal or a window or something. You probably heard the guards talking about where we would be taken," Lucas said.

"But…" Marvin said quietly. "No. I'm sure I saw it. The light didn't glint off glass. There isn't any glass in the windows. It was Morse code. It told me where you were."

"Suuuuure it did," Lucas said. "I think you need some sleep, buddy."

Marvin sat perfectly still, deep in thought. *If Lucas didn't send that message, who did? What in the world was that light?*

12

Thanks to the horse and cart, they arrived at half-past eight in the same town they had visited earlier in the day. Louis explained that he didn't want to go to the village, just in case they were being followed. He also didn't want to put Pierre and his family in any danger. Instead, they would spend some time in an abandoned building that was once the blacksmith's shop. Louis knew how to get into the building. He used to hide there many times when he was a child.

They decided to hide there while they formulated their plan. Then they would take the horse and cart to the forest beyond the castle.

Everyone sat around the darkened room. Even though it was summertime, the August night had a slight chill to it. Marvin wasn't completely convinced that it was the air. It might have been the chill running through his bones at the thought of the upcoming battle.

"Hey, Lucas. Do you want to hear about our big discovery?" Nicole asked.

"Bring it on. Nothing would surprise me right now," Lucas answered.

Nicole looked at Louis, and he nodded. Then she spilled the beans. She told Lucas all about Louis and the cave and the portal.

Lucas' mouth hung open in disbelief. "No way," he said.

"Way," Nicole answered.

Lucas stared at Louis for a moment. Louis looked a bit uncomfortable. "Wow. So…what year did you disappear?" he asked.

Louis shook his head. "I am not certain. For some reason, I think it was 1734. That is the date inscribed on a coin that I have. It must be the year I left. I have always wondered about that coin…"

"Wow, sorry to see you didn't make it back. At least you weren't gone forever. I mean, you still exist," Lucas said.

"*Oui.* I did not know how to get back. Nicole and Marvin have explained everything to me," he said. "I just wonder what my real home is like."

They sat quietly for a few minutes, trying to think of something to say to Louis to make him feel better. "Sorry you vanished into a wall and never saw your family again" didn't seem to cut it.

Finally, Louis broke the silence. "That is enough about me. For now, we need a plan. What are we to do next?"

"We *were* supposed to spy on Mr. LeClair to get information, like what time he's leaving the castle and if he is bringing anyone with him. We might have even found out what route he's planning on taking. That way we could have stopped him before he even got to the King," Marvin complained.

"Yeah, well, you were kind of busy saving my neck," Lucas said.

"Ha ha," Nicole scoffed.

"Anyway, we know LeClair is going to the King's forest. We know it's happening tonight. Calm down. There's no need to lose your head," Lucas joked.

"Okay. We get the point," Nicole said.

"After all, we can figure it out. Two heads are better than one," Lucas continued.

"Yeah, yeah." Nicole rolled her eyes.

"Okay. Forgive me. I don't know where my head's at today," he said.

"Enough with the head jokes!" Nicole finally shouted. "That was serious. You were minutes away from death, Lucas. Now stop talking about it like it was a big joke."

"I knew you cared. Give us a kiss," he said jokingly. He closed his eyes and made fish lips with his mouth.

"Lucas, you are impossible!" she scolded. She folded her arms and rolled her eyes. "Does anyone have something serious to say?"

"Yes, I do," Marvin said. "Since we didn't gather the information about Mr. LeClair's plot against the King, we have to think of another plan."

"Wait, Marvin, I got some information from Jacques." Nicole quickly filled the group in on what Jacques had told her.

"Okay," said Marvin, "here's what we know: Mr. LeClair is going to attack the King in the King's forest; the battle is happening near the river; and it's happening two hours past sunset, when the history books say the King forded the river and entered the royal forest. I think we should go early, hide, and then wait. Then, we send Jacques out for the initial battle with Mr. LeClair, and we distract him so Jacques can…"

Lucas cupped his hands and used a deep voice. "Destroy him."

"No, we aren't going to destroy him. We just want to stop him," Marvin corrected.

"Whatever that means," Lucas mumbled. "The guy's going out there with one thing in mind, and he'll be armed."

"It means we want him alive. It means we don't want to have someone's life on our conscience. It means…" Nicole was getting worked up.

"I get it. It means that no matter the threat we face, we face it with respect for life. Even if someone

else resorts to violence, we try to win without it,"
Lucas stated. "I'm cool with the non-violent thing."

"Can we stay on topic here?" Marvin said.
"Anyway, Jacques will go out first, then we distract
Mr. LeClair, allowing Jacques to knock him from his
horse. That's when Louis comes in. He runs out,
taking his sword just to make sure Mr. LeClair can't
recover his weapons. Then Jacques helps Louis hold
him still, we tie him up, and *voila!* We've captured
the imposter."

Nicole translated the entire plan to Jacques,
who nodded thoughtfully.

"And if he does not lose his weapons when he
falls, I will do what I must do," Louis added.

Marvin sighed. "Let's just hope things go the
way we've planned. It's the best we can do."

Jacques spoke to Louis and Nicole.

"Jacques said that the imposter has formed a
small army. He has planned that most of them will
leave tomorrow to find Gutenberg and destroy his
printing press. The others are to stay behind."
Nicole paused. "What if the imposter brings a small
army with him tonight?"

"Then it's game over," Marvin said gravely.

They talked a while about the possibility of
Mr. LeClair bringing a small army, but the reality
was, as far as they could tell, no one else in that
entire castle, including his closest bodyguards,
knew that he was not the real King Charles VII. Not
even his wife, who lived in another part of the

castle and had little to do with him. Not his son, who was also away at battle. Only Jacques, known as Jacques Coeur, who was the King's argentier, or personal treasurer, knew of the switch—and he found out by accident. That was why he was thrown in prison for "knowing too much." That was why he was supposed to have been executed.

As far as they could tell, Mr. LeClair merely stepped in, assumed the role of king, and started getting rid of anyone he felt might get in his way. Jacques and Louis agreed that this imposter had confided in no one, and so he couldn't very well bring an army along with him. A group of soldiers would be too risky. If even one high-ranking person or church official found out, the fake king would be finished. They were pretty certain he wouldn't risk it. Besides, Mr. LeClair knew from the history books that King Charles VII was returning from battle in northwestern France and would take a certain route back to the castle.

Jacques spoke again in French to Louis, who turned to the group. "Jacques said we do not have to worry. The King always travels with a small army to protect him. He will not be alone."

"Not this time," Marvin answered. "According to our books, King Charles VII was captured by the enemy at the end of the battle and locked away. He managed to escape, but he was alone. He will be coming back to the castle with no protection this time."

Louis translated this to Jacques, who nodded his head, a look of concern on his face.

Marvin started wringing his hands. It was almost time to leave for the forest. "So we're agreed then? Everyone will stick to the plan?" he asked.

Everyone nodded. Marvin sighed. He checked his watch. It was nine o'clock. If they wanted to get to the forest early, before Mr. LeClair, they had to leave now. Jacques said that Mr. LeClair's plan was to attack the King at two hours past sunset. And sunset had been at eight o'clock.

They left the abandoned blacksmith's shop through the loose boards that served as a back wall, crouching to squeeze through. The horse and cart were tied up out back. Louis looked around carefully. The night was still and quiet. They climbed into the cart while Louis took his place on the horse. In the moonlit night, they ventured off toward the forest.

Every bump made Marvin's heart jump. The land was so rough that he almost fell out of the cart along the way. In fact, he almost hoped he would. Although he had faith that the plan would work, Marvin couldn't stop his mind from racing. He kept questioning himself, asking why he was risking his life to save some king that meant nothing to him. He wondered what he would do if he got caught in the forest and couldn't make it home. He took a deep breath and let the air out slowly. Then he closed his eyes and tried to listen to the voice deep down inside, his inner voice. When he listened to his inner voice, he felt better. This mission was something he had to do. It was the right thing to do. History depended on it. Learning and equal rights depended on them saving the real king before the imposter king could destroy the Gutenberg press. Marvin shook his head and looked out into the darkness.

Time flew by, and before long, they were entering the King's forest: the forbidden forest.

Owls swooped overhead as they entered the thickly wooded forest. It was damp and dark, and Marvin noticed that the sounds of this forest were different from the sounds in the woods at home. As they rode deeper into the woods, Marvin could hear the loud, rushing sound of the river. When they reached the water, they climbed out of the cart. Louis dismounted and unhitched the horse from the cart. Jacques would need it to battle Mr. LeClair.

Jacques and Louis walked around the area near the river, talking. They came back and explained that, since Mr. LeClair would be coming from the castle to meet the King near the shallow bend of the river, the fight would most likely take place in the clearing next to the river.

Louis pulled the cart into a thicket to hide it. Then he led the horse near the thicket and tied it to a tree. He petted the horse's nose and fed it some oats from his pocket. He was very concerned that the horse be treated right. He wanted to make sure it would not run away or get too excited when Mr. LeClair arrived.

"Mr. LeClair will likely enter the forest from there," Louis said, pointing off to his left. "The King, as you have said, will return from Cherbourg along the river, over there," he added, pointing straight ahead and to the right. Then, Louis pointed out a large mound of bushes where they could all hide. It was at least thirty feet from the riverbank.

Louis grabbed a stick and scratched a plan into the ground, marking where they would hide, where the horse was tied, and how Jacques would ride in. He dragged his stick along the ground to represent Mr. LeClair, and then King Charles VII. They all could see how the plan was supposed to work.

Marvin patted his knapsack. He didn't have his trusty flashlight, but he had brought a few other things. He wasn't allowed to have them. But he had saved them from his neighborhood's street party, knowing they would come in handy. This one time, he was going to do something very dangerous.

Marvin looked at his watch. It was nearly ten o'clock. "Okay, I think we should hide now. Sunset was at eight o'clock tonight, and LeClair is supposed to attack the King two hours past sunset. And I don't really want to be surprised by a guy who might show up early. Especially since he's the one who might have a bow and arrow."

They all took their places behind the bushes. Marvin thought about it for a minute, and he realized that he had been hiding and sneaking more in the past few months than he had in his whole entire life, including the year in grade two when he and Lucas used to play hide-and-seek for hours. It was a funny feeling to be hiding from danger all the time. And it really didn't feel good.

Suddenly, he couldn't wait to go home. But they were far from finished, and far from home.

13

They waited quietly near the bank of the river. The night was silent, except for the dull rush of the water and a few frogs and crickets. There was barely a breeze to stir the leaves. The air hung heavy like a thick fog, and billowy clouds in various shades of gray moved across the sky like a curtain. The moon was slowly being blocked by the clouds, but it seemed to fight for its rightful place in the sky. The battle between the dark clouds and the amber moon kept Marvin's attention.

"I hope we are able to save King Charles before the storm," Louis whispered. He looked up into the dark sky and took a deep breath.

"There doesn't seem to be any wind or anything. Maybe we won't be getting the storm after all," Marvin said. He reached under the back of his tunic and grabbed his watch. It was ten o'clock now. Show time.

"There is always a calm before the storm," Louis said. "It is your chance to prepare. It is nature's way of giving you a moment to brace yourself for what is to come."

Marvin thought about that as they sat quietly in the bushes. No one moved. No one spoke. They were perfectly still. But any minute they would have to fight with all their might. It was the calm before the storm.

As he sat in the darkness, Marvin could feel his heart beating in his chest. Would their plan work? Would they be hurt? Would they make it back to the castle on time? But his heart was pounding for another reason, too. He was about to come face-to-face with a medieval king, a figure he had read about in history class and who had been a part of important historical events. It was the chance of a lifetime, and Marvin was sick with excitement. No one in the world today could say they had met King Charles VII. Except Mr. LeClair. And he didn't count.

Jacques was the first person to spot the weary soldier in the darkness. He gasped and pointed, and when the moon came out from behind a cloud, they all could see the King approaching. He hardly looked like a king. He had no cape and no crown. Instead, he wore battered armor, and some of the pieces of armor were missing. His beard was long and scruffy, and his messy hair fell down around his shoulders. He trudged along pitifully, like a wounded animal. He did not look injured, but he looked beaten. He had no horse to carry him. There was nothing at all in his hands. A bow and arrow were strapped to his back.

"That's King Charles VII?" Marvin asked doubtfully. He squinted his eyes to focus on the dirty figure in the dim light. Marvin had been looking forward to this moment, the day he would meet the real King Charles VII in the flesh. Now the King approached, but he didn't look like a king at all. He didn't look important.

"That is him," Louis said, his face shining.

Marvin could tell that Louis was happy to see his king. Just as Louis was about to rise from their hiding place, however, Jacques grabbed his arm and pulled him back. When Marvin looked off in the other direction, he realized why Jacques had stopped Louis. Mr. LeClair was riding a white steed, galloping toward them at full speed. He was cloaked in black, and he carried a lance. A long sword was sheathed by his side.

As he got closer, Marvin noticed that Mr. LeClair was wearing armor, but he wasn't fully clad. Pieces were missing. His hair fell loose and messy, and his face was unshaven. Marvin blinked a few times. It almost seemed that the King was going to have to fight *himself!* Marvin also noticed one other thing. There was someone else sitting on the horse, behind Mr. LeClair. Marvin wondered why Mr. LeClair would bring his backup with him on the same horse. *Wouldn't it be better to bring along another knight on his own horse with his own weapons? Why would they share a horse?* he wondered. But it was obvious to Marvin that Mr. LeClair was expecting a fight. And he was going to get one.

The wind kicked up and the sky grew gray and angry. Thunder clapped from a distance and birds scattered through the treetops. For a brief moment lightning lit up the sky, casting a garish light on the King and the forest. All of nature was preparing for a storm.

They waited for the right moment, like they had planned. Mr. LeClair looked around the woods. He seemed to be looking for someone, even though the King was straight ahead.

Upon seeing Mr. LeClair, the King raised his hand and smiled. *Poor King Charles,* thought Marvin. *He thinks someone has come to help him.*

Mr. LeClair stopped and stared at the King in the distance. His horse reared up on its hind legs and whinnied. The man sitting behind Mr. LeClair struggled to get free from what looked like ropes tied around his wrists.

That's weird, thought Marvin. *He brought a prisoner along with him. And it looks like one of the prisoners who escaped the beheading today.*

Marvin snapped out of his trance when Mr. LeClair raised his lance straight out in front of him, preparing for an attack. The King stopped walking, his smile fading with the realization that this knight was not here to help him, but to spear him. Just as Mr. LeClair's horse started to charge, Jacques went into action.

He mounted the brown horse that waited patiently in the woods and then galloped toward Mr. LeClair. Jacques pointed his lance outward, ready for the taste of armor. They had agreed that they would try to capture Mr. LeClair without harming him, but in a battle it was anyone's guess what would happen.

"Stop in the name of the King!" Jacques shouted into the dark night.

Mr. LeClair slowed his horse and turned to Jacques. He smiled a nasty grin and shook his head.

"There you are, you snake. You escaped your beheading and made it here, I see. It is just as I suspected. Where are the others?" he asked.

"What others?" Jacques called, still ready with his lance.

Mr. LeClair laughed a wicked, throaty laugh as thunder crashed in the distance. "I know who helped you escape. Where are they now, the cowards? Hiding, I would bet. That is just as well, I suppose. I will conquer you all. Look around this forest. It will be your grave site," he growled. "Marvin, look who I have brought along to see you. Come out from your hiding spot and say hello to your friend."

Marvin's breath was caught in his chest. He focused his eyes on the prisoner on the back of Mr. LeClair's horse. The hooded man turned toward the bushes where Marvin crouched. The bright blue eyes and friendly face were unmistakable. Marvin couldn't breathe. He couldn't move. His head started to spin, and his stomach started to churn. He thought he was going to throw up.

"Grandpa Dave," he said in barely a whisper. He was about to jump up when Lucas grabbed him by the arm.

"Marvin, don't," Lucas whispered. "Keep to the plan. If you come out now, he'll go after us and fight us all first. Let Jacques take care of things first, and let us do what we came to do. You can't run headlong toward the enemy. It would be death for all of us."

"But...my grandpa..." Marvin stuttered.

"I know, buddy. But it doesn't change anything. Stick with the plan. It's our only hope of winning," Lucas whispered sternly.

Lucas' tight grip on Marvin's arm was painful. He wasn't sure if the pain was causing his eyes to water or if it was something else.

Mr. LeClair still did not see where they were hiding. "Fine. Then you will stay hidden and watch your grandfather suffer!" he shouted. The horse reared and Mr. LeClair charged toward Jacques, their lances pointing straight ahead. Jacques' lance grazed Mr. LeClair's armor, and the lance fell to the ground. Mr. LeClair laughed. "Ha ha!" he cried. "Losing so soon?"

Jacques unsheathed his sword and raised it high in the air. He turned his horse around to take another pass at Mr. LeClair. Mr. LeClair pointed his lance and charged. Jacques knocked the weapon out of his hands with his sword. Thunder crashed again in the distance, and a flash of lightning lit up the sky. The horses circled back around to face off once again.

"When I am done with you, Jacques, *old friend*, I will get rid of the rest, including my prisoner," Mr. LeClair yelled.

The King tried to load his bow with the two remaining arrows he had at his side. He was so weak that he could barely pull back the bow. The arrow zinged through the air, narrowly missing Mr. LeClair.

Mr. LeClair pulled out his sword as Jacques approached him, and didn't notice when his prisoner fell from the horse, landing with a hard *thud* on the ground. Marvin watched Grandpa Dave writhing on the forest floor. If he didn't move, he would be trampled or speared. Marvin's heart was burning in his chest. No matter how much he wanted to run to help his grandpa, he had to stick to the plan.

The clanking sound of metal filled the air. Jacques swung his sword with both hands, thrusting the heavy weapon toward Mr. LeClair.

Thunder crashed as the imposter and Jacques battled. Suddenly, Jacques was hit and he flew off his horse. The horse ran away as Mr. LeClair galloped toward the King, who was waiting like a sitting duck in the forest. The King was out of arrows, and out of energy. Marvin was certain that this would be the end of King Charles VII.

Suddenly, a clash of thunder sent Mr. LeClair's horse into a panic, rearing up on its hind legs. Mr. LeClair fell off, but he didn't seem hurt. He leapt to his feet and ran toward the King, brandishing his sword. A single blow to the head sent the King to the ground. Mr. LeClair gave a shout of triumph. Then he raised his sword and prepared to attack the King again.

Marvin held up a small item that he had fished out of his knapsack and lit it with a match. When he threw it in the air, sparks of light and loud popping noises filled the darkness. Mr. LeClair turned, looking wildly around the forest for the source of the light show. His horse, which had been standing nearby, reared up and whinnied, then took off into the forest.

Marvin concentrated on trying to light the second, and last, firecracker. He threw it into the air, covering his ears as the stick burst into loud crackles and pops of light. Then Mr. LeClair looked toward the bushes. Marvin stood up. Raindrops fell from the sky as Mr. LeClair grinned through the darkness.

"You are next!" he shouted at Marvin. He left the King for the moment and raised his sword high into the air, his maniacal laughter filling the forest.

Just as he was about to charge at Marvin, Jacques recovered and ran over to intercept him. Suddenly, rain began to pour and lightning lit up the sky. Jacques and Mr. LeClair battled. The clash of metal echoed the clash of the thunder. Lightning flashed as Jacques swung his heavy sword and sent Mr. LeClair flying. When it was over, two men lay on the ground almost side by side.

❧14❧

Jacques stood over the two men. He had his weapon ready, just in case Mr. LeClair got up to fight again. Nicole and Lucas burst out of the bushes and rushed to his side.

Marvin ran over to his grandpa. "Are you okay?" he asked as he bent down to check on him.

Grandpa Dave sat up and shook his head for a minute. "I'm fine. A little bruised and battered, but I'm fine," he said.

"You didn't tell me you knew about the portal," Marvin said.

"You didn't tell me, either. When I found out that you were using the portal, too, I decided to follow you. You lost a coin, you know," he said.

"But...where have you been going? How long have you been here?" Marvin asked.

"Oh, Marvin, we have a lot to talk about," Grandpa Dave answered. "I've been using that portal for years, but I've never been to medieval France before. Not until I found your coin...and found out you had been using it, too. Hey, you got my message, huh?"

Marvin didn't know what he was talking about. He hadn't heard any message from his grandpa before he left. He thought for a minute and then suddenly it hit him. "The S.O.S. Of course! That was you! Thanks!"

"My pleasure," Grandpa Dave answered. "Thanks for the flashlight. I couldn't have gotten along without it." He handed Marvin his small blue flashlight.

Marvin stared at him for a second. "Wait a minute. That means you were one of the hooded prisoners we rescued from the tower! When did you get captured? What did they lock you up for?"

Grandpa Dave looked sheepish for a moment. "I've been on my own mission, Marvin. Once I got here, I realized something that you probably don't even know. Mr. LeClair was planning a siege on Britain. A great battle was to come in a matter of months, and Mr. LeClair had weapons hidden away. I have been trying to find the hidden weapons and convince his advisors of the terrible consequences, but they wouldn't listen to me. That's when I got locked up. Thanks for the rescue, by the way."

Marvin was still confused. "But then why didn't you get in the cart to escape with us? Why didn't you tell me? Didn't Lucas know that you were one of the prisoners with him?"

Grandpa Dave put a hand on Marvin's shoulder. "No, he didn't know it was me. I kept quiet and listened to Lucas and Jacques discuss the plan you had for Mr. LeClair. I figured that if I had revealed myself to any of you at that time, you might not have got away so quickly. I didn't want to hold up your escape or get in the way of your mission. Besides, there was no more room in the cart! I was planning to get my hands on a horse of my own and meet you in the forest, but I got caught again," he said.

"But Grandpa, you should have told me. What if you hadn't got away the second time?" Marvin asked, disappointed.

"Marvin, trust me. I did what I thought was right. I had got myself into a terrible mess, and you kids helped me out of it. On our next mission, I'll be more open and honest with you," he said.

What mission? Marvin wondered. Grandpa Dave walked away before Marvin could ask him any more questions.

They quickly made their way over to the King and the imposter, who lay on the ground. Neither man was moving.

"What happened? Did Jacques hurt him?" Marvin asked Louis.

"He was not wounded by the blade of the sword. He was only hit and went down from the blow," Louis answered.

"Ouch. That can't feel good," Marvin muttered.

"Uh oh," Lucas said, looking at the lifeless bodies on the ground. "Are they...?"

"I don't know," Marvin answered. "But we have another problem here." He looked from one man to the other. Neither had a weapon. Both were dirty and soaking wet. Both had blood on their faces and in their shoulder-length, scraggly hair. Both had unkempt beards. And both were partially dressed in armor. Marvin looked back and forth, but he couldn't tell which was which.

Is the teacher dead? Is the King dead? If we have killed the King, are we dead? Marvin wondered. If the wrong man lived, he would throw them in prison. If neither man lived, they would have to answer to the guards and nobles of the castle. Either way, it was bad news.

Nicole bent down to the man lying closest to her. She put her ear to his mouth and grabbed his wrist. "He's alive!" she said.

Lucas checked the other man. "He's alive, too!" he called.

For a moment they were relieved. Then they realized they had a problem. Although both were alive, how would they know which one to tie up on the way back to the castle?

Even Jacques couldn't tell which was which. Lucas looked closely at both men. Then he smiled widely. "I can tell you who is the real King Charles VII," he said.

"How?" Marvin asked.

"You can tell from their cheeks," Lucas said.

"What?" Marvin asked. The men looked the same to him.

"The tiny scar on the left cheek. That one is Mr. LeClair," Lucas announced. He pointed a finger at the man lying to the left. The other man began to groan and reached for his head.

"Lucas said the same thing the last time, when we saw Mr. LeClair in the castle. He was right then. I still can't see that scar very well," said Nicole, shrugging her shoulders. "No matter how much I bug Lucas about not paying attention in school, the guy notices every detail and can pick it up a mile away. Amazing."

"I heard that!" Lucas said. He ran his hand through his short, red, spiky hair. "I knew you thought I was amazing!"

"Oh, brother," Nicole groaned. She rolled her eyes and walked over to the man they now knew was King Charles VII. Although he was alive, he didn't look good. Blood trickled from a gash in the side of his head.

Lucas and Marvin ran back and forth between the river and the bleeding king. Louis took off the white shirt he wore under his tunic and tore it into pieces to make washcloths. He and Jacques kneeled beside the King, trying to make him comfortable. They didn't have a bowl or a bucket, so Lucas and Marvin kept soaking the pieces of cloth to clean the King's wounds. Nicole quickly removed her apron and tore it into strips. Then they wrapped the long, dry strips of cloth around the wound and tied them tightly to stop the bleeding.

Jacques and Louis had both brought along leather flasks filled with water, which they took from their hideout in the town. They shared first with the King and then with the others. Marvin tilted his head back, held the flask above his lips, and dribbled the clean water into his parched mouth. He hadn't even noticed how thirsty he was until the water slid down his throat. He swallowed the water and sighed, wiping his mouth with his shirtsleeve. Lucas took a drink, and then he brought the flask over to Nicole.

Nicole was standing a few feet away. She was standing guard beside Mr. LeClair just in case he was faking his injuries, even though everyone else was certain that he was thoroughly unconscious from his fall.

When the King's wounds were attended to and he was able to stand up, Jacques asked Dave, Lucas, Marvin, and Nicole to give him a few minutes to explain things to the disoriented king. Louis walked away with the others, but Jacques stopped him.

"No. You have the right to be here, too. Stay and help me explain to the King what has happened," Jacques said in French.

Marvin sat with his back to a tree. He didn't care that the ground was wet and muddy. He was incredibly tired. Grandpa Dave, Lucas, and Nicole stood beside him. They watched as Jacques and Louis spoke to the King. The King embraced both men, and they led him toward the others.

Marvin jumped to his feet. The King stood in front of them, a tired smile on his face. "How can I thank you?" he said in almost a whisper. Marvin felt proud and also amazed at what was happening before them. Marvin felt a well of excitement building in his chest. He had known he would be excited to meet the King. He just wasn't prepared for the awesomeness of it all. Chills ran up and down his body. He had spoken face-to-face with King Charles VII!

Louis was able to round up the horses and bring them back to the river's edge. They helped the King onto Mr. LeClair's horse. Then they went back to the unconscious Mr. LeClair, dragged him over to the other horse, and draped him across the back end. Mr. LeClair looked like a pathetic saddlebag. Jacques stood between both horses, took the reins, and led the group through the trees to the open field that led to the castle.

They walked a long time before anyone spoke. The King was the first to break the silence, and he spoke for a while to Jacques in French. Occasionally Louis would join the conversation, but it was clear to Marvin that Louis was in awe of the King and was not entirely comfortable being around him. Marvin began to wonder if Louis had ever been in the King's presence before. *Maybe the closest he ever got was being at the jousts and helping Sir Jean the Fierce*, he thought.

Nicole, on the other hand, was not intimidated by the King at all. Marvin had wondered how long it would take for Nicole to join the conversation. She was a girl with opinions, and she was not too shy to share them.

"You know, what you did to Joan of Arc in 1431 was terrible," Nicole said. She kept walking and looking straight ahead.

The weary king looked at her with narrowed eyes. "I did nothing to Joan. She helped me win the battle of Orleans. She was captured by the English and burned at the stake. I did not harm her," he answered quietly.

"But you didn't help her. I mean, you wrote one letter to the King of England to set her free. That's all. She helped you win back France from England. She helped you become the King of France when everyone else wanted Henry VI of England to become King of France."

Lucas elbowed Nicole and gave her a warning look. Marvin was worried, too. Although they had helped save the King from death by imposter, they were still in danger of angering him or raising suspicion.

The King stared straight ahead, too weary to argue with Nicole.

"Anyway, how awful to be burned at the stake as a witch. What a terrible name to be called. And now she will be known forever as a witch," Nicole said.

The King looked at her with confusion. "Do you really believe that she will be called a witch forever? People will forget. Years from now, no one will remember why she was killed, just that she helped the King and was killed by the English. Her reputation is not tarnished."

Marvin gave Nicole a warning look. She was in danger of giving away too much information.

"All I can say is that even though you couldn't save her, the least you can do is make it right. Make sure everyone knows what a wonderful person she was. Make sure that everyone remembers her not as a witch, but as a brave, supportive woman who helped France," Nicole said finally.

"Enough!" the King yelled. "I am tormented by the memory of the girl. I do not wish to speak of this any longer. I cannot do anything for Joan of Arc now. It is too late."

"It is never too late to make things right," she said quietly.

"Silence, child, or you will be punished," he said firmly. He stared straight ahead. Nicole finally got the picture and stopped talking. She lowered her head and marched on silently.

Mr. LeClair stirred only a few times, slumped over the back of the horse. It let them know that he was alive. Other than that, Mr. LeClair was out cold, his hands and feet bound with rope just to be on the safe side.

After about an hour of walking, they could finally see the castle up on the hill near the horizon.

❧ 15 ❧

The guards at the gate looked confused to see the King, tired and dirty, riding with commoners. He was not riding with the Scots Archers, and he did not look dressed for a ride in the woods.

The horse and the crew went across the drawbridge and stopped at the doorway. At first, the guards simply stood at the entrance to the castle, blocking the way. They didn't move aside, but they didn't come forward in attack, either. Then they noticed Mr. LeClair on the back of the horse. A few of the guards reached for their weapons.

"*Écartez-vous!*" the King bellowed, the big voice coming from nowhere. They were startled. He hadn't spoken in more than a weak, quiet voice since they met him. The guards moved aside to let the parade pass.

Six men dressed in red tunics ran quickly toward them as they helped the King off the horse and dragged Mr. LeClair to the ground.

"Sire!" they exclaimed, a look of disbelief on their faces. *Qu'est-ce qui c'est passé?* One of the men took the horse to the stable. Two of the others suddenly noticed Jacques and Louis. They moved forward forcefully in an effort to seize them. The King's voice bellowed once again. The guards backed off like puppies.

"What did he say?" Lucas whispered to Nicole.

"He said, 'leave them, or it is your head,'" Nicole answered. "Then he told them to summon all the Scots Archers and the highest ranking officials of the castle to meet in the library."

Moments later, the sound of trumpets filled the air. Marvin figured it was the call to the officials. They had to have some sort of system for emergencies. No one had a cell phone!

Marvin checked his watch. It was eleven o'clock. They didn't have much time before they would have to leave. He looked nervously at the others, but Lucas and Nicole shrugged their shoulders and followed the King up a few flights of stairs. Marvin tried to help Grandpa Dave up the stairs, but not for long.

"Marvin, what do you think I am, old?" Dave whispered, pulling his arm away.

"No. It's just that you hurt yourself falling off that horse. I figured—" he started to answer.

"Well, forget it. I'm fine now. All I needed was a good stretch. I'm almost as fit as you guys, you know," Grandpa Dave said, smiling.

Louis disappeared through a doorway, but joined them a moment later with a clean new shirt in his hands. He buttoned the shirt as the group climbed the stairs and entered the library. The room was lined with beautiful books. It was crowded with lords, nobles, advisors, and bodyguards. When the King entered the room, some of them gasped at the sight of him, still dirty, bruised, and bloody. A sea of shocked faces stared at him.

Lucas, Marvin, Nicole, Jacques, and Louis stood near the windows. Grandpa Dave leaned casually against the wall, as though he belonged in the room as much as anyone else. Marvin smiled as he watched his grandpa speak French to some of the nobles around him. Grandpa Dave was in his element. He looked truly happy.

Marvin looked around, admiring the rich velvet curtains and the embroidered wall hangings. Dark wooden shelves lined the walls. On a shelf beside him, Marvin found a collection of coins in a wooden box. They were from all over the world and looked to be from many different years. Grandpa Dave inspected them briefly and said that some were hundreds of years older than the one they had from 1450! Heavy, carved wooden chairs were placed throughout the large room, but today, no one was sitting down.

The King addressed the room in French, with Jacques at his right-hand side. Everyone listened intently as he spoke. When he snapped his fingers, guards brought in Mr. LeClair. He had woken up from his unconsciousness and was raving like a madman. The crowd gasped again and then began to whisper amongst themselves. One man stepped forward and asked the King a question. The King held up his hand, and Jacques spoke briefly.

"What's happening?" Lucas whispered to Nicole. She was watching with wide eyes. She did not take her eyes off the scene in front of her, but she turned her head slightly to answer Lucas.

"The man asked how they know for certain which man is the real king," Nicole answered.

"Well? What did he say?" Lucas asked.

"He didn't say anything. He held up his hand to the crowd. He's wearing his royal ring with his seal etched into it. Then Jacques told how the imposter had locked him away and planned to do away with the real king. He said they were both saved by a brave squire," she answered.

Then the guards dragged the screaming imposter from the room, to be locked in the dungeons. As he left the room, Mr. LeClair fixed his icy green stare on Marvin and laughed. He pointed his finger at him but didn't say anything. Then he disappeared around the corner.

Marvin shivered. "Okay. That was freaky," he said quietly.

Lucas turned and made a strange face at Marvin. "Yikes. I wouldn't want to meet up with him ever again," he said.

Suddenly, all eyes were on Lucas, Marvin, Nicole, and Louis. They stared back in silence. Marvin was worried. Had Louis told them about the time travel thing? Was the crowd going to turn on them?

"*Viens ici,*" the King said loudly to Lucas, Marvin, Nicole, and Louis.

"He said 'Come before me,'" Nicole translated, sounding nervous.

They inched hesitantly toward Jacques and the King.

"For your bravery in battle and saving the life of the King of France, I grant you my favor," the King said in French. Nicole translated.

They stood wide-eyed and perfectly still as Jacques left the room and came back seconds later carrying a burlap bag and a beautiful, shiny sword. Large jewels were set into the carved hilt of the sword. Marvin wondered if the King was going to give it to Louis.

"The King wants to present you with gold coins from his treasury," Jacques said. Lucas, Marvin, and Nicole looked at each other. They couldn't believe it. Marvin figured there was a fortune in gold coins in the burlap bag.

They looked uneasily at one another. Marvin knew exactly what they were thinking. They didn't come on this adventure to get rich. Besides, they couldn't very well show up in modern times with a bag of gold. How would they explain it to their parents? How would they ever cash it in? They whispered back and forth for a few seconds as the King watched them questioningly.

"Sir, if we may, we would like to present these coins to Louis to share with his friend in the village who helped us," Nicole said in French.

The King looked shocked. So did Louis. "As you wish," the King said. He handed the bag of coins to Louis and turned back to the others. "Then how will I repay you?" he asked.

Marvin smiled. He pointed to the coin collection on the shelf of the library.

"You don't need to repay us at all," Nicole explained. "But if it pleases the King, may we have a coin or two from your collection?"

The King glanced over to the shelf where the collection sat. Some of the people in the room started to laugh.

"But those coins are worthless. They have been collected by my father and myself, but they were minted in the time of their rulers. They are of no value now. You cannot use them for payment," the King explained.

Nicole translated to her friends. They discussed his offer. Then she turned back to the King. "That's okay. We would treasure that collection above all else," she answered.

"Then so be it!" the King announced. One of the guards went to the shelf and removed the wooden board on which the coins were mounted. Marvin grinned and raised his eyebrows at Grandpa Dave.

"But I am not finished with you," the King bellowed to Louis. Louis looked worried. Marvin wondered if the King had found out about Louis sneaking in and out of the castle. Louis did not move a muscle, and did not say a word.

The King told the people crowded around them now to back up, and then he spoke quietly to Jacques. Jacques' face slowly lit up with a smile. He handed the sword to the King.

"Although you have not spent an entire night in the chapel, as is customary, I feel this is the time to reward your bravery. Louis, please kneel," the King said.

Louis looked around the room in bewilderment. Marvin's jaw dropped open.

"For your devotion to the King, and to France...for your bravery in battle...for your skill and faithfulness...I hereby knight you," the King announced. He tapped the glittering sword on each of Louis' shoulders. Then he raised the sword high in the air. "Arise, Sir Louis the Brave!"

Louis stood up, a look of pure joy on his face. His eyes sparkled as the King handed him the beautiful sword and Jacques placed a red tunic on his shoulders.

Marvin felt a lump in his throat. He looked at Nicole, who was wiping a tear from her eye. Lucas was smiling.

Lucas looked over at Nicole. "It's okay, Nic. We can get you a red cape, too. You don't have to cry," he teased her. She slapped his arm but didn't say a word.

After Louis had been congratulated over and over again, Marvin, Lucas, and Nicole rushed over to talk to him. They stayed and talked to Jacques for a while, and eventually told their war stories to others in the room. The only part they left out was the part where they appeared through the wall. As far as everyone else in the room knew, Lucas, Marvin, Nicole, and Grandpa Dave were from Britain, just like they had told Louis months before.

It turned out to be quite a party in the library, and Marvin didn't want it to end. Servants brought food and drinks from the kitchen. Lucas, Marvin, and Nicole didn't realize how hungry they were until they started to eat.

Marvin almost forgot to check his watch. When he finally looked, it was nearing midnight.

"We've got to go," Marvin said. Lucas and Nicole sighed.

"I'm coming with you," Louis said as they left the library.

Marvin waved good-bye to King Charles VII, the King of France, and shook his head. *This kind of adventure will never happen to me again*, he thought.

He clutched the wooden board of coins under his arm, went across the room to get Grandpa Dave, and followed Louis, Nicole, and Lucas down the torch-lit hall one last time.

⚜16⚜

When they got to the dungeons, they quickly changed back into their regular clothes and went down the hallway where the portal was located. Grandpa Dave asked Louis a million questions on the way.

Even the damp, dank smell of the dungeon didn't bother Marvin. He tried to soak it all in so that he would never, ever forget it. They walked to the end of the long stone hallway to await midnight and go home.

Nicole looked back sadly at Louis, who was checking one last time down the other hallways to make sure no one saw them. Even though they had helped save the King, they didn't want to risk getting caught disappearing into the wall. There was still a risk that someone would try to stop them. And Louis still had to live with the consequences.

"Nic, get a grip. You can't stay, and he can't come with us. Louis is not boyfriend material. Besides, he is training to spear people. You're the one who is always against violence on T.V. You must see the irony of this," Lucas said.

"Hey, he's only doing what he has grown up with. It's not like he's a murderer or something. He only battles to protect the kingdom or protect his honor," she said. She had that glazed look in her eyes again. She was staring off into the darkness.

The boys just shook their heads.

"Besides," she said, "I know he can't come back with us. I'm not stupid. I've just never met anyone like him before. I'm really going to miss him, that's all."

Lucas and Marvin looked uncomfortable. Lucas picked up a stick and held it in front of his mouth. He pretended to be an announcer. "That concludes today's episode of *As Time Passes*. Be sure to tune in next week as Nicole falls in love with a seventeenth-century pioneer."

"It could happen," Marvin said.

"Oh, stop it," Nicole said. "I don't have a crush on him. I just like him as a friend—like you guys. It's just too bad we'll never see him again. It's too bad he lost his chance to go home."

A moment later, Louis walked back down the hall toward them.

"Maybe. Maybe not," Lucas said. He held several coins out in front of him. One of them had the date 1743 on it.

"Where did you get that? It's from two hundred years later than the King's year," Marvin said.

Lucas smiled at Grandpa Dave. "Someone else who collects coins just gave it to me," he answered.

"This isn't the right year, Lucas. He left the forest in 1734, not 1743," Nicole said.

"I know, but that was nine years ago. He can't go back to the year he left. He was only five years old. Look at him now," he answered. "This coin will take him back to nine years after the date Louis left the forest."

"But he can't go. He didn't go back within twenty-four hours," Nicole said. "Right?"

Lucas shrugged his shoulders. "Maybe you have to make it back within twenty-four hours for *that* trip. But this would be a whole new trip. Who knows? This is a whole new coin."

Louis took the coin from his hand and looked at it for a long time. "So this is the coin that can take me home?" he asked.

"If you got the year right, that is the coin that should take you home," Lucas said.

"But Louis, you were younger when you disappeared. Now, you're fourteen years old. Your parents might not recognize you. They might be…" Nicole didn't finish her sentence.

Louis hung his head. "They might be frightened. I know. And I don't even remember them. But if I go back, they will look the same. I will know them when I see them. At least I have to try."

Lucas walked over to Louis and slapped him gently on the back. "If you decide to use it, I hope it works for you, man. And I wish we could see you go. If you do make it through, I hope you find your parents. Maybe you should take this along, just in case." He handed him the coin from 1450. "That way, you can always come back here. And for the record, this is our number. Give us a 'call' if you ever need us." He handed Louis another coin. It was one from modern times.

Louis smiled. Marvin checked his watch. Three minutes to go. He nodded to Nicole, Lucas, and Grandpa Dave.

Grandpa Dave stepped behind Marvin and held on. Lucas wrapped his arms around Grandpa Dave's waist, and Nicole grabbed hold of Lucas. Marvin held his hand with the coin to the wall and waited. He looked back at Louis and smiled. Lucas and Nicole looked back one last time, too. No one had the heart to say good-bye.

Seconds later, the wall started to light up. Marvin closed his eyes and held tightly to the wooden board with the coins in his left hand. As the swirling light got bigger and bigger, he got ready to step inside. Even though he wanted to go home, a part of him felt heavy with sadness.

When the light was a huge circle, he took a deep breath and stepped out of the dungeon for the very last time.

❧17❧

The ground was cold against Marvin's cheek as he lay there. Lucas, Nicole, and Grandpa Dave climbed to their feet after a hard landing. Marvin was almost getting used to being totally squished in a goose pile. He stood up and looked around the familiar cave. *It's funny how so much can be different, but nothing has changed,* he thought.

As they walked into the forest, Marvin clicked on his flashlight.

"Home sweet home," Lucas said. He breathed in deeply and smiled.

"Yeah. It's good to be home," Nicole said. Neither of them sounded totally convinced.

"I'm sad, too," Marvin said quietly. They all smiled a little.

"Hey, do you think we did it?" Lucas asked.

"What do you mean by that? We saved the King, didn't we?" Nicole said. She tripped over a rock and almost fell.

"Careful there, Nic. First day with the new feet?" Lucas asked. Nicole made a *tsk* sound. "Anyway, obviously we saved the King, but we might have changed history by doing that. I mean, Louis got knighted, LeClair got locked away, and everyone in there saw us. Who knows? Maybe we set off some other little ripple in time. Maybe we changed things anyway," he said.

They thought about that for a few moments as they marched through the dark woods. There was no way of telling whether anything had changed yet. They wouldn't know if the world was the same as they left it until they got home.

When they got near the forest entrance, Marvin stopped. He shone his flashlight on the wooden board. He looked at the coins, which were mounted with melted wax. He counted twenty-three coins, all from different countries and different years. Lucas, Nicole, and Grandpa Dave stopped behind Marvin.

"You know what we could do with those?" Lucas asked. He raised his eyebrows knowingly. Grandpa Dave and Marvin smiled.

"Oh no. That's it, you guys. No more traveling through that portal. We are not going to use those coins for anything. Now let's get out of here. I just want to go home," Nicole said.

Lucas, Marvin, and Grandpa Dave smiled a little as they walked out of the forest, but their faces soon grew concerned. The streetlights were out. Marvin thought it was odd that all the lights on the street were out—even the ones in the houses.

"Uh oh. Maybe things did change because of us," Marvin said.

They walked a bit faster as they continued down the street. Marvin looked left and right. The houses seemed to look the same, but it was hard to tell. There was no power. He started to think the worst. *Maybe we changed history, instead of saving it,* he thought. *Maybe what we did was just as bad as what Mr. LeClair did.*

All Marvin wanted to do was get home. Then he saw his parents.

"There you are!" his mother called, running over to them. "The power just went out on the street. I went to see if you were okay, but you were gone." She hugged Marvin, then wagged her finger at him. "You should know better, young man."

"Hi, Mom," Marvin said, smiling. "I was just… um…out with Grandpa for a second. There's a star formation you can only see at midnight. We just couldn't miss it."

"Well, next time you plan to meet the kids outside in the middle of the night to look at planets or stars, you ask permission. And that goes for you, too, Dad," she said. Now she wagged her finger at her father.

Grandpa Dave shrugged and put his hands in the air. "Guilty as charged," he said. "Sorry, dear. We're just a couple of adventure seekers."

Mrs. McKnight smirked a little. "Yes, well. I don't know how much adventure you'll find looking at rocks and studying the stars, but you still need permission to be out at night. Got it?"

"Got it," Marvin answered. He hugged his mom one more time before she went inside to get her keys. She insisted on driving Lucas and Nicole home at such a late hour, even though they only lived a minute away.

"Nope, nothing has changed," Lucas said.

Before Marvin's mother came back outside, they gathered in a circle. "Thanks, guys. This would never have been the same without you," Marvin said. He put his fist out. Lucas made a fist and put it on top of Marvin's. Nicole and Grandpa Dave added their fists to the pile. Suddenly, the streetlights buzzed and flickered back on. The whole neighborhood was back to normal.

Mrs. McKnight jingled her keys and got into her car. Lucas and Nicole didn't say anything. They just smiled and broke away from the circle. Then they got in the car and pulled the doors shut.

Grandpa Dave and Marvin watched as the car pulled away, and then they walked up the lawn toward the house. "Well, I've got to go, Marvy boy," he said. "Maybe we can get together and go rock hounding next week?"

Marvin smiled. "Sure, Grandpa," he answered. Grandpa Dave turned around to walk to his car, which was parked on the street. "By the way, some day I want to hear all about it," Marvin called. Grandpa Dave raised his hand in a wave and disappeared into his car.

When Marvin turned around, he almost climbed up the trellis to get into the house, but this time the door was wide open. He went upstairs, closed his bedroom door, and flopped on his bed. Then he sat up and started picking the coins off the board. When he had a pile, he reached down and opened his bottom desk drawer. He pulled out the small wooden box and placed the coins inside. The lid would barely close. *Now that's a collection,* he thought.

He put the box back inside the drawer and stood up to close his window. Somehow, he couldn't do it. He left the window open and looked out into the dark night. The fresh scent of nighttime filled the room, and he climbed into bed.

He thought about the wild day they'd had, and their amazing experience in the forest. He thought about Louis and wondered if he would ever go home. As he dozed off he thought about the guards...and the King...and Lucas, dressed in tights...he was riding a pink horse...and carrying muffins...

The adventure begins!

Part one of the exciting medieval series

The Mystery of the Medieval Coin

by A.D. Fast

There is something very strange about the social studies teacher at Green Park Elementary School. When Marvin, Nicole, and Lucas follow him to the ancient cave in the forest, they discover a secret. Now, they must stop a madman before he changes history forever. Can they do it—without losing their heads?

For more information, visit
www.tealeafpress.com

TEA LEAF BOOKS

ENCOURAGING RELUCTANT READERS

EXCITING STRONG READERS

INSPIRING A LOVE OF READING

Spend the summer with Mel Randall and Will Bergeron! The novels in the **Deer Lake** series follow the summer cottage adventures of two young teens and their group of friends.

The **Nate's Journal** series gives readers a glimpse into the life and times of eighth grader Nate Brown—through his own humorous personal journals.

See all our titles at:
www.tealeafpress.com
or call
1-800-661-6136

Selected teachers' guides available.

Special Thanks

Many thanks to Susan Roberts and Ron Fast for their editing and translation work. Sincere thanks, as always, to my Tea Leaf partners: Jane Lewis, Heather Evoy, Kate Calder, and Hannelore Sotzek.

Sincere thanks to Ben Kooter and Vanwell Publishing.

One wonderful teacher and several students helped shape this story, from writing their own sequels, to drawing sample covers, to reading the entire manuscript and noting their edits. Watch for books in the future from these up-and-coming authors. A heartfelt thanks to Susan Plat-Lindsay and her class of creative students:

Samantha G.	Colton W.	Kendra D.
Amber S.	Danielle D.	Courtney D.
Sam M.	John K.	Emma L.
Connor P.	Emily W.	Callum J.
Reed E.	Jared U.	Ben A.
Tessa F.	Luke F.	Abiye M.
Alex P.	David O.	Tyler D.
Paula A.	Elizabeth G.	Greg G.
Meagan C.	Rachel K.	Daniela C.
Kaitlyn B.	Emma B.	Savannah S.